I0569769

OTZI
THE ICEMAN

By

Bud Seligson

Lost Age Publishing
2017

Otzi the Iceman © 2015 Bud Seligson

All rights reserved. No part of this book may be reproduced or transmitted in any form or by any means, electronic or mechanical, including photocopying, recording, or by any information storage and retrieval system, without permission in writing from the Author.

The following original novel has been filed and registered with the Writers' Guild of America, West, under the name of Bud Seligson.

Originally Published by The Zharmae Publishing Press, (November 8, 2015)
Printed in the United States of America

Cover Art and Interior design by: Cyrusfiction Productions.

Second Edition Paperback
ISBN: 978-1-946480-12-5

9018 Balboa Boulevard
Suite #562
Northridge, CA 91325

Dedications

To my wife Diane,

    If I listed all the many ways that you have helped me, this dedication would be larger than the novel.

—all my love, Bud

Table of Contents

OTZI

THE ICEMAN

By

Bud Seligson

Prologue

Otzi "the Iceman" was a man living in the Alps mountain region between Austria and Italy in the so-called Bronze Age. In 1991 Otzi's mummified body was discovered by a hiker near the summit of Mount Similaun in Austria. The body was preserved beyond any plausible expectation because for five millennia it had been encased in glacial ice. The Alpine glacier had retreated in recent times, leaving Otzi's body exposed. Although the corpse's body fat had wasted away over time, Otzi's skin and clothing were intact. Examination of Otzi's body shows that he had sustained an arrow wound to his left shoulder, which may have contributed to his death. Otzi was well armed and had, two hours before, dined well on ibex, or mountain goat.

Scientific analysis has revealed many details about Otzi the Iceman's manner of life. Scientists and researchers will continue to pore over this information in an effort to better present a picture of the ancient man's life and times. The author of the present volume has relied on another source of inspiration: that is, the testimony of a friend. This friend of the author claims to have received much information in a series of dreams on consecutive nights. The worthy woman believes, without a shadow of a doubt, that these dreams were sent directly to her by the Moon Goddess, Perchta. The author reserves judgment on the accuracy of these visions. His purpose merely is to transcribe these bits of information, and to let the public decide.

The Ceremonial Kula

"Tell me again, Ajax—have we lost our love for the mountains of our home?" asked Otzi, leader of the Thuringia Tribe, as he and his friends walked along a dusty road in the lowlands of what is now Italy.

"Not at all, O tribal leader," replied Ajax, Otzi's right-hand man. "The Moon Goddess, Perchta, commands, and we would be foolish not to obey."

"What has happened in the past to those who have disobeyed?"

"Not much, O Otzi. The Eisenthaler Tribe, neighbors of ours, neglected their duties to Perchta. An entire mountain collapsed upon them one day, leaving them buried beneath rubble."

"Sounds unpleasant," replied Otzi with a half-smile, though obviously, it was no laughing matter what had happened to the Eisenthalers.

"It was for them, I'm sure," replied Ajax with an answering smile. "Though they are not around to tell us so."

The plains stretched out on either side of them, far

and flat to the south and away from the mountains. The horizon shimmered in the day's heat. The white grain swayed in the breeze, grew still when the breeze lingered, and then swept to one side again when it resumed. The path was broad and traveled by many leather-shod feet. A fine dust coated and buffered the travelers' footfalls from the firmer clay beneath.

The walking party was five strong, selected to represent the tribe at that summer's ceremonial Kula. The Kula, amongst peoples of central Europe in the year 3000 BC, was a gift-giving ceremony held in honor of the gods. On the occasion tribes exchanged "Kula Rings," or ornamented discs. The exchange and the ceremonial feast were demanded of tribes by the gods. The augurers left no doubt as to that point. In former years Otzi and the other members of the Thuringia Tribe had gone to nearby villages in the Alps Mountains. These had been pleasant occasions, if modest. This year a messenger had arrived in Thurin Village bearing an invitation from one of the lowland tribes. The mountain folk had never been to a lowland Kula and were intrigued. They accepted the invitation.

The road was lined with tall cedar trees. On one side rose up a scrubby hillside, tufts of grass and bushes, pines and the occasional broadleaf tree. The cedars provided some shade. First in the group was Otzi, dark haired, sturdily built, and of just about the medium height in those days. His face was rugged and intelligent. On his chin was a rough, short beard. His eyes were a piercing shade of blue. Otzi was guileful and shrewd. He had survived a hundred adventures and expected to survive a hundred more. At the ripe old age of thirty-four, Otzi was the undisputed leader of the mountain-loving Thuringians.

Next to him as they walked was Ajax, taller than Otzi by an inch or two. Ajax's hair was dark and his muscles strong. Ajax honed his body through constant exercise. His skin was smooth but the firm sinews and muscles stood out beneath it. The muscles of his arms bulged when he clenched his fist. Like all those who lived at high altitude, he was not often short of breath. His chest, barrel-broad, was a taut vellum of hardened muscles. Long could he endure in these lowlands, for his lungs were used to contending in the thinner air of the heights. He would always have this advantage over the flatlanders. Ajax was going to compete in the Kula boxing competition, and he was confident of doing well.

A few steps behind him was a Lemnas, a young lad, agile and blond, who carried hitched to his belt a complement of heat-forged copper throwing knives. Next was Artemis, a tall and dusky-blond girl, an archer with high cheekbones and a stern, imperious look. In her agile fingers, she twirled one of her arrows as they walked. Its point was hardened copper, while in the back cropped hawk's feathers served as fletching. Slung over her shapely shoulders Artemis carried a long yew bow. Last but not least, particularly in years, was Nestor, a gray-bearded man with a staff. Nestor was hale, enduring, and fleet of foot though his years numbered not less than sixty.

The day was warm and the mountaineers were not used to the heat. They felt though that they were not far from their destination and they kept up their swift step. Otzi gazed out over the rippling grain to the south. Here was unlike the mountain valley they had left a few days before. They had been cheered on their way by the villagers. Some of the young girls threw Alpine flowers down on their heads from the houses. The traveling party had laughed and protested, but they enjoyed it anyway. The flatlands were warm and broad. Life here seemed not as keen but more welcoming. Otzi pulled a stem of wheat as they walked. He broke off the root and put the stem in his mouth. The flatlands made a nice change, and he liked adventure.

Ahead of them on the road they could see another party, numbering seven or eight. They too would be going to the Kula. Their destination was the hall of Trilock the Magnificent, a potentate in these parts. Many tales were told of the headman's festive table. He was leader of the Autharia Tribe. Trilock's hall was on Autharia Island in the middle of Lake Donoma. Lord Trilock's lands included the island and the area ringing the lake for several miles.

The road bent slightly to the right. They could see beyond the hill on their right more hills, steep and forested. The trees here were largely broadleaf, a lighter shade of green than the conifers of Thuringia. In back of them were snowy mountains, miles and miles away—the Alps. They were of a height comparable to Thuringia but the outlines of these mountains were unfamiliar to Otzi. Otzi and company had walked south for three days, then east for another three. Now a broad stripe of blue water came into view. This would be Lake Donoma. The shore was not far now.

"How much do we know of this Lord Trilock?" asked Artemis of the others.

"Not much, when all is told," replied Ajax. "We have heard stories from people who pass through Thuringia. Many tribes are in league with him, while others do his bidding. The messenger suggested that Trilock would have important words for us at the feast."

"We have our Kula Ring?" asked Nestor apprehensively

from the back. "We haven't dropped it on the way?"

"Nope, got it here." Otzi thumbed toward his backpack.

"Although, as I don't have to tell you, Elder," put in Ajax, "the Ring is not for Trilock. It is for Perchta."

"No, you don't have to tell me that," rejoined Nestor wearily. Ajax's devotion to Perchta was strong, sometimes inflicting boredom upon his friends.

"Try telling that to Trilock the Magnificent," put in young Lemnas with light mockery.

The others chuckled.

"Well, I can't wait," put in Artemis, nodding. "I want to test my skill against these flatlanders."

"The competition will be stiff," said Ajax.

"The more the better," replied Artemis, with unsmiling pride.

"It should be interesting," commented Otzi, reflecting upon the event as a whole, as befit his superior age. "We'll hand over our gift, in hopes that Perchta does not bring the mountain down upon us in the coming year."

Autharia Island

L ake Donoma was several miles wide and many miles long. Steep forested hillsides ringed it around, while the blue fringe of water continued out of sight to the south. The travelers ahead of them stopped at the fringe of the lake. Here was a landing, a little wooden platform and shallow, gravelly beach. There were two people to greet them, a man and woman. A boat pulled up to the wooden platform. The travelers got into the boat and it pushed off the landing. The boat was long, narrow, and sleek. On either end its hull rose in a high, graceful curve. Several rowers helped to convey the vessel away at speed. Its destination was about a mile hence, the shore of an island. The water chopped into small and active waves in the afternoon breeze.

Otzi and his party approached the landing. The attendants welcomed them smilingly. They were tall and elegant in dress and demeanor. They wore their long hair pulled back and carefully combed. The Thuringians were impressed with the greeters' dress, for it was of shiny fabric not found in the mountains. The garment was a single long tunic, tan in hue, and embroidered at the shoulder with gold stitching. Otzi and his friends wore animal skins to ward off the mountain cold. Beneath these they wore rough, loosely woven cotton shirts, while their legs were clad in soft, undecorated leather. The difference between the flatlanders and them was striking.

A second boat approached the landing.

"Are we among the first guests?" asked Nestor of the greeters.

"No, sir," replied the lady greeter. "People have been arriving since last night. By the evening fully one hundred-and-fifty people should be in attendance."

Ajax raised his eyebrows in wonder. The boat pulled into the landing and the greeters wished them an enjoyable Kula. The boat was constructed of a light-colored wood. Horizontal slats were lashed together and caulked with a black, pitchy substance. The interior was lined with an attractive blond wood. There were benches at which sat strong rowers. A broad tan sail hung slack from the mast. The rowers pulled away from the shore. One of the rowers got up and opened the sail. The wind filled it and they moved quickly toward the island. The ski was bright and white small clouds lay clustered across it.

As they grew closer, the visitors could make out features of the approaching shore. Autharia Island was large—perhaps a mile or two long, and half a mile wide. It had been landscaped: the side facing them was a garden, and off to one side was a broad green lawn. This lawn, they guessed, would be the site of the athletic contests. The fringe of the island was trimmed and edged with a walking path. In the middle of Autharia rose a low hill, on top of which was Trilock's lodge. Here was a sprawling, clay-colored building, expertly designed and handsome to look upon. A pathway led up some steps that came to the lodge's main entrance.

The boat arrived at the dock. Here stood two more greeters, also dressed in tan. The Thuringians stepped out. There were directed up the cut-stone pathway toward the house. To the right on a patch of green stood dancers in billowy dresses. With graceful, swaying gestures they welcomed the guests to the island. The travelers climbed the steps to the landing. In the forecourt was a tall and elegant woman with dusky, smooth cheeks and lustrous auburn hair.

"Welcome, Otzi and friends," said she. "I am Sincha of Leponto. We are very happy that you could attend. Please, this way."

The mountaineers followed in the wake of the hostess, Sincha. On either side of the lodge grew shapely cedar trees. The front of the lodge was high and proud: square pillars on either side of the door rose to a height of twenty feet. The visitors were impressed.

"You have come, I understand, from a long way off?" Sincha asked Otzi over her shoulder.

"Several days' journey, yes. Much of it, however, was downhill," added Otzi, with a sally of self-deprecating humor. Sincha and the others smiled.

"The lofty mountains are your home," observed Sincha with a smile. "How I should like to visit them one day."

"You will be most welcome when you come," replied Otzi.

"Travelers have come from even greater distances. With us now is an ambassador from a land called China."

The travelers murmured their interest in this news. Sincha led them into the hall. It was as grand inside as on the out. They walked to one side, down a dim hallway, and came to a broad door. This opened onto a suite consisting of several rooms. In the center was a living area in which they might relax.

"This evening," concluded Sincha, "you shall perhaps hear much of interest. The third bell will announce the beginning of the Ceremonial Feast. Welcome to Autharia."

The others bowed courteously to their hostess, who bowed in return and left them. They looked about the suite. The furnishings were well made and comfortable. On one side of the rooms was a line of windows faced with clear glass. Otzi and the others were impressed with all of this, which was so different from their own village. Thurin Village could boast none of these refinements, and the Thuringians considered importing one or two of them when they returned to the mountains.

In the bathing room were urns of water with which to bathe. When they had refreshed themselves, servants brought food for their lunch. The mountain folk looked with amazement upon the assortment of fruit, bread, cheese, and thinly sliced chicken breast.

"Nice," commented Lemnas, who was hacking together a sort of sandwich. "Yeh," said Ajax, putting his big fist around a handful of grapes.

"But the cheese? I'm not excited about this stuff," objected Nestor. The others laughed. Nestor liked to have something to grumble about, even when his complaints bordered on the ridiculous. Such was the case here. Nestor cracked half a smile knowingly. The cheese was far beyond the humble goats' curd their own village could offer.

"Yes. Very disgusting," put in Artemis.

"Don't eat too much, remember, Ajax," cautioned Otzi. "You'll be no good for the boxing tomorrow."

"Don't have to worry," Ajax jabbed a wad of chicken in his mouth.

"We need you mean and chippy as ever."

"I will be," said Ajax.

The travelers found comfortable beds and dozed off for a few hours.

The hostess, Sincha of Leponto, moved silently through the halls of Lord Trilock's lodge. The passageway was broad and airy. On the walls hung woven decorations and clay stelae, upon which were drawn elegant figures in vegetable and animal-derived pigment dyes. Burning censers lit the halls where there were no windows. Sincha walked into a section not used by guests. There was little traffic. She opened the door to a large room without knocking. This was the suite of Trilock himself. Tall, robust, and broad-shouldered, Trilock faced the window. He did not turn around. "They have arrived?" he asked.

"They have," replied Sincha in a low voice.

"Tell Zeras," he commanded. "But tell him to be careful. We can't have them getting suspicious."

"Yes, sir," replied Sincha in a deferential tone, and withdrew.

The Ceremonial Feast

The ceremonial gift, or what we have called the "Kula Ring," was to be presented at the beginning of the Kula feast. The Thuringians' Ring was a particularly splendid example of the form. At the mountain heights in which Otzi's village lay, valuable and brilliant gemstones were often in plain view. The Alps Mountains were sharp and chiseled. Bel, the Earth God, so the tales went, had been particularly angry with his wife, Aveta. In a fit of rage one day he had grasped with his hand a large portion of the Earth's crust. With a single mighty shake, he had pulled up the mountains that now rose to such towering heights. Gems that would have lain hundreds of feet beneath the surface suddenly came into view.

Larissa, one of Thurin's village elders, was a master craftsman and artist. The Ring was a circular band, forged with copper and tin and about ten inches wide. In this band Larissa had etched delicate patterns. The metal was polished and was set with greenish gems, in the modern parlance called titanite. When she was finished, she presented it for the village to admire. They acclaimed it as her best work to date. The villagers of Thuringia might not have all the fineries of those of the lowland. They might not eat dainty foods and wash three times a day in the warm waters of Lake Donoma. The Thuringian Kula, however, was second to none, and all those in Trilock's hall praised its beauty.

The Thuringians had changed out of their travel gear. Now they wore linen blouses, leather leggings, and sandals. They had combed their hair, adding to it, after considerable hesitation, some of the bath oils furnished by the lodge. Artemis and Lemnas wore their hair pulled back, while their elders had let theirs hang shaggily loose.

"You're all pretty," commented Ajax, when he saw the neatly dressed Otzi emerge from his room.

"Shut it." growled Otzi, who grinned after a moment. Otzi was unused to these refinements and a bit worried that it made him less of a man. He laughed this off, however. In a day or two he and the rest of them would be back to their unkempt selves.

They left their suite. In the halls were ushers who pointed them in the right direction. The broad halls were filled with other guests going to the feast. The parties were of widely varying appearance.

The central dining room was a large, rectangular room. Glass windows on one side admitted the light of the early evening. The sun had gone down behind the mountains. The sky was a deep and luminous blue. As the shadows lengthened, the guests could see a group of fishermen in the distance taking in their haul.

Tables formed a broad rectangular ring, leaving the middle of the room bare. On one end was an open space with a low platform. The speaker, standing on this, would rise a few inches higher than those around him. The tables were laid with tablecloths of a shimmering whiteness.

Elegant bronze tableware was set before each chair. Otzi and his crew were led to places next to one another. There were, in all, more than a hundred-and-fifty people in attendance. The mountaineers looked with wonder upon all the types arrayed here. Some were fair and pale-skinned with flaxen hair and long, clean limbs. These people Otzi had met before, for they passed now and again over the mountain pass of Thuringia. Dark-skinned men and women also occupied a prominent place. Otzi guessed that these were from the south, where the harsh sun had burned their skin a darker color. These people were tall and elegant, wearing cloaks of bright red, purple, and yellow. Others, rustic and brawny, sat in conversation with their neighbors. They did not look unlike Otzi, although their skin was more olive hued and their hair dark almost to blackness. There was, near the head of the table, a man noticeable even amidst these proud folks for his haughty expression. This man wore the tan-hued clothing common to the household, although his was covered by an armored leather vest. This was Zeras, head of Security Affairs for Autharia. Zeras ate and drank little throughout the meal.

The hall was loud from the guests' conversation. Otzi sat next to a man with a frank, calm manner. He was richly dressed, wearing his smooth hair swept back from his forehead. His features were regular and pleasing, broad and open, although behind his eyes one could catch a hint of shrewdness.

"My name is Lorran," this man announced, in reply to Otzi's inquiry. "Otzi," replied the foremost Thuringian.

"Ah, so I have the pleasure of speaking with Otzi," said Lorran. "This name is known even to us coastal people."

"Is that so? How surprising," replied Otzi modestly. "Which coast are you from?"

"The eastern. I am from Mastaan," said Lorran. This was a town that lay at the top of the sea separating Italy and marking Italy's eastern border.

"A place not unknown to me as well," replied Otzi.

"Your town lies on an important trade route. Salt mines have opened up in the north. If travelers go over the Thuringian Pass, they save themselves a journey of many, many miles."

"There are other ways over the mountains," replied Otzi with a self-deprecating smile.

"But none," countered Lorran, "so low in altitude that one does not find oneself deep in snow. Yes, we know something of you Thuringians," replied Lorran with a grin.

"We welcome your custom," said Otzi with a nod. "We ask but a small fee for your passage. Bring with you a pelt, a coin, or a token expressing the pride of your homeland. We shall be happy to let you pass."

"Sounds fair to me." Lorran nodded in turn. "Everything must have some price. Mastaan values its independence, as I'm sure do you. We maintain it by charging a fee for the transport of goods. With such largesse we're able to protect ourselves from our neighbors. Not that we don't trust them," assured Loren with a smile, "but we don't trust them."

"Caution," said Otzi with an understanding nod. There came the tap on a bell and the audience turned their attention to the front of the room. The sound of conversation died down. Up on the platform stood now a large man with red hair and a commanding presence. He wore the same tan clothing but also a sweeping cape and a bejeweled necklace. This was Trilock, master of Autharia and host of that year's Kula ceremony. Next to him was a table upon which stood a white goblet. It was a very singular-looking object: Otzi could not guess of that which it was made.

Trilock had long red hair and a full, florid face. His expression was proud but also not without humor. He smiled now at the assembled guests. He held up his hand for attention.

"Greetings, travelers," he began. "We are very pleased to have you at our Kula Ceremony. We are very thankful for your Ceremonial Gifts—given, as we understand, not to us, but to the great gods up above in the sky. We hope that you are in a celebratory mood. Tonight, we feast; tomorrow, we will watch with great attention the athletic events which are to take place. This gathering, like all Kulas, promotes understanding between the tribes, between the lands. Some of you have traveled just a short way; others, a great distance. With us here is a traveler from the Far East. He has been here several days already, and in this time has told us such things that have made our eyes pop out with wonder. May I present Lao-Tse, Ambassador from the land of China!"

The guests shouted loudly their welcome. The Ambassador was a thin man a little above the ordinary height. He was dressed in an outfit of blue and white. He looked like no one Otzi had seen before: his eyelids were narrow and his skin drawn handsomely tight over his face. He had broad cheekbones and cheeks tanned dark by the sun. His skin was of an unseen golden hue, and his expression reserved and proud.

Lao-Tse bowed his greeting to the guests.

Now Trilock resumed. "O distinguished guests!" he cried. "We have much to learn from one another. Through close cooperation we can help each other to greater ends.

For too long have we worked to frustrate each other's ambitions. Of the many good things to come out of this meeting, let cooperation be foremost."

He lifted the white glass from the table. "Distinguished guests, trade is much on our minds. Now, I ask you, what is the foremost item of trade amongst the peoples? Is it not salt? By means of this wondrous substance we can preserve our foods beyond all expectation. We can help our bodies to remain healthy. Last but not least, we can achieve a level of cooperation not previously dreamed of.

"This goblet, wrought of salt mined from far-distant hills, may serve as a pledge to our lofty purpose." He snapped his fingers. Two servants came up. On one side a man poured into his glass a greenish liquid. This turned out to be lime juice. The other poured out a smaller quantity of yellow-tinted drink. This turned out to be alcohol made of fermented cactus. With a smile Trilock lifted the glass made of salt and took a sip.

"Hmmm. Delicious," he said. The attendees laughed and clapped. And they dined.

Lorran of Mastaan sat at a table with one of his men. They were playing a board game involving pebbles of two different colors, black and white. The board was a painted grid of equally sized squares. Each player took turns putting down a pebble. The goal was to overcome one's opponent's line of pebbles. Whoever overcame more of the opponent's pebbles won. Ordinarily, Lorran felt great enthusiasm for the game. This evening he was preoccupied.

Lorran was a keen observer of the relations between

men. Long had he observed the realms on the flatland plain. Many of these realms' merchants had to come to Mastaan to transport their goods. Lorran had met many men like Trilock over the years: ambitious, expansive, and heedless of obstacle. He had suspected that the Kula would be about matters other than the ceremonial gift giving, and the feast had confirmed him in that. There was a tingle in the air, and the presence of that Chinese Ambassador seemed to be one side of it. What did Trilock and men have in store? Lorran was skilled in strategy and did not want to be caught off-guard. Something told him that he and his men would not be the object of the Autharians' attentions. He thought back over the evening. His neighbor, Otzi, had been interesting and unexpected. Stories were told of these mountain men, but one did not expect to see one face-to-face. Would Otzi be caught off-guard, he wondered. The mountaineer had less experience of the flatlanders' wiles.

Trilock's partner made a skillful move in their game.

"Looks like this one's yours," Lorran nodded with a grin. He rose, made himself a drink, and walked out on the verandah to look out at the view.

The Games

"How did you like Trilock?" asked Lemnas later that evening when they were back in their rooms.

"He was all right," replied Otzi nonchalantly. He had not himself been to an event anything like this size, but he was a man of the world. Many adventures had Otzi been through in his thirty-four years. From the intensity of conversation Otzi sensed that something important was happening at this Kula. The speech of Trilock had had significance for more than a few of the tribes. No doubt they hoped to profit by the trade in salt, which Trilock was promoting.

"I didn't like him," pronounced Artemis, with an air of distaste.

"Oh? Why not?" Ajax was folding and unfolding a leather fingerless glove. This glove would play a role in tomorrow's festivities. He seemed to want to soften the leather by bending it back and forth.

"He did not seem genuine."

"He's complicated," replied Otzi. "He has lots of fish on the grill."

"Be that as it may," insisted Artemis. "Something's a little slippery."

"Hmm, maybe," replied Otzi.

"Well," added Ajax, stretching and rising from his chair. "Perhaps the events of tomorrow will reveal more."

The next day the attendees gathered at the arena for the athletic competition. A number of events were taking place that day. Some would finish that same day, while others would conclude the following day. Wooden benches had been set up for the guests. Trilock appeared in a low flowing robe. Sincha was not far behind him. The islanders again wore outfits of a matching color, except that today they were magenta rather than tan. Trilock chatted with the Chinese Ambassador, explaining the rules and asking how they differed from those of games in his country.

The events included archery, foot races, the hammer throw, knife and javelin throws, boxing, and wrestling. Three of the Thuringians were taking part. Lemnas had stripped down to a short tunic, lightweight cotton shirt and sandals. Artemis wore something similar. These two lithe figures earned appreciative glances from the audience. Ajax stripped to the waist and wore, over his hands, the same leather fingerless gloves of the evening before. Ajax would be competing in the boxing event.

The high-Alpine air of his home benefited Lemnas in the running event. His lungs were more powerful than those of the flatlanders. He came in third in the middle-distance run, which was in length one loop around the island. Two slender dark-skinned runners from the south confided to him that they, too, came from the mountain uplands of their land. They outdistanced Lemnas by a hundred paces in the race. Lemnas excelled at knives, and later that day he would participate in the knife throwing. Meanwhile Artemis took part in the archery competition. She came in first in her half of the draw. The event would finish up the following day.

The boxing ring was filled with contestants. These men stood in assembly in a circular ring before the crowd. The first battle had been between smaller men. As these men stalked around the circle, they hit each other with a hundred blows. The punches did not do much damage individually, but with the minutes they began to tell. One fight was stopped because one man's eyes had closed with swelling. He could no longer see clearly. The less-damaged man triumphed to much applause.

Next up was Ajax. The Thuringian stood before the contestants and the spectators. The proud-looking second-in-command under Trilock was acting as a manager to several boxers from Autharia. This was the man called Zeras. Zera was tall and rugged, and his face was proud and unyielding. He looked Ajax scornfully up and down.

"Mountain-born hick! You don't give yourself a chance, I'm hoping."

"Maybe I do," replied Ajax with a defiant smile.

"So much the worse for you," snorted Zeras, who nodded toward his contender.

A man called Gunkar came forward. He was very big, with limbs and shoulders knobbed with long-developed muscle. Ajax was big, but Gunkar was a brute. A bell rang and the match began. Gunkar started fast, moving to the center of the circle. He swung relentlessly with his brawny arms. Gunkar delivered a fierce blow to Ajax's midsection. Ajax partially turned it away with his forearm but it still glanced his kidney. He winced in pain but dodged away as the other man came at him. The other man, confident of success, swung mighty blows coming forward. Ajax ducked beneath these and delivered three short body blows to the passing man. This hurt the other man, who turned and pulled up his arms. They circled each other in the center of the circle. The man shot out a jab which caught Ajax painfully in the ear. Then Ajax countered with an overhead right. He followed it up with three more blows in quick succession. The bruiser might end the fight with one shot, but Ajax was proving himself to be quicker.

Zeras snarled at the bigger man to rush forward. Ajax fended off this attack and rolled off to one side. Zeras protested that this was not in the rules. The judge waved his appeal away. Once more the big man rushed forward and this time Ajax jabbed him twice in the lower back, where the kidneys were. The man leaned over in pain. Just as he was turning again Ajax was on him. He delivered several fierce blows to the head. The big man pushed him back and swung wildly but he was hurt and fading. He did not move as quickly; the kidney shots had taken his legs. This time Ajax moved in without fear and punched him in the sternum. He hit him below the jaw and again on the forehead. The man staggered back; two more punches and Ajax had finished him. The man fell to the dust. Zeras shouted out in rage.

Otzi clapped as Ajax waved victoriously to the crowd. Sincha came up to him. "Otzi, you do not compete?"

"Let the others have their fun," said he, with a self-deprecating smile.

"All the others?" replied Sincha suggestively. "We want to have fun too." Otzi glanced at the woman who stood next to him. She was as tall as he, confident, yet smiling demurely. Her auburn tresses swayed gently in the wind.

"The island is interesting. You must enjoy it here."

"It is many things," replied she. "Here it is very busy, of course, very festive. But there are quieter spots as well, where the birds do nothing but sing all day."

"Lovely," replied Otzi. Otzi was by no means immune to Sincha's charms. He was a married man, with a devoted wife back in the village. Ana was his light, his rock whenever things became difficult. Sincha here was something Otzi did not often encounter: a flatland woman, warm, curious. She was a very pretty woman, with firm, dusky skin and a high, sculpted bosom. Her neck was shapely and slender.

"I'm showing the Sarwanians around in a few minutes. If you'd like please tag along," she said a brisk, neutral tone.

"Sounds good," replied Otzi with a nod.

Zeras looked across the boxing circle at where the villager Otzi stood. He was talking to Sincha, he noted, *The little tart!* he thought to himself. Zeras was beside himself with annoyance at the defeat of Gunkar. The mincing smiles of Sincha, which left little to the imagination, irritated him, if possible, even more. But then Zeras took hold of himself, reflecting upon the events of that very evening. He smiled, very slightly, to think of the changeableness of fortune. He glanced at Trilock, whose expression was one of unvarying good humor. Trilock chuckled at something the Chinese Ambassador had just related to him.

The attendees celebrated their victories. They thanked Trilock and the islanders for the excitement of the competition. The games would continue the following day. Sincha crowned the victors with wreaths made of juniper twigs. As they were walking back to the lodge,

Lord Trilock walked close beside Otzi and his friends.

"My compliments to your land and to your athletic prowess!" said Trilock cheerily.

"Thank you, Lord Trilock," answered Otzi in turn. "It's all that fresh mountain air."

"Indeed? Zeras was less than pleased. Now, now, my dear friend," he chided. Zeras, who was not far off and could hear the conversation. "Fair is fair, and this Ajax has fists of stone."

"He's a tough one all right," conceded Zeras, with a rictus of a grin.

"In a few moments the Ambassador will tell us something of the land he's from. He was, just think of it, one hundred-and-eighty days on the road to get here!" Trilock's eyebrows drew up in a show of astonishment. "He says that villages in China number not hundreds but thousands of souls. Only he doesn't call them villages. He calls them *cities*." Trilock moved on to another group of guests.

⚔

The center of the island was wooded and peaceful. The trees were deciduous and in full leaf. The Sarwanians spoke in a language Otzi did not understand. They were a handsome, compactly sized people from over the Great Sea. They looked up at the mighty elms and beeches of the islands and gasped. "He's saying that he would like to bring these trees back to his land," translated Sincha, who had locked her arm through Otzi's as they walked.

The Sarwanians talked amongst themselves and admired the grove of tall trees into which they'd come. Otzi thought of Ana and felt a twinge of guilt.

"You are thinking of your wife?" asked Sincha with a knowing smile.

Otzi chuckled and said nothing. This Sincha took for an affirmative response.

The Sarwanians had melted away into the woods. Now there was no sound but the breeze above and their steps as they walked.

"In the mountains" Sincha said wistfully, "there is Otzi's heart."

"No," said he, lightly. "I take it with me always. It is needed for courageous tasks."

"Very necessary, I'm sure," said she. She gestured at a grassy bank which rose above the path. They climbed to it and sat down. Otzi felt the warm body of Sincha next to him. She was young and yet seemed sad, constrained. He did not quite understand her. Sincha reached up her narrow hand to Otzi's chest. Without a further word she leaned in and kissed him.

"Mountain man," she murmured, and kissed him again. Otzi did not respond to the first kiss, but responded to the second. This Kula was proving to be unlike any he had been to before. He reached his arm around her waist and pulled her toward him. Sincha's breath was becoming heavier. The Sarwanians were long gone. There was a bell far in the distance. He could feel Sincha's frustration. She cursed softly, then pulled herself away. She rose silently.

She looked back at him with a smile. "What are you doing tonight?" she asked, and walked away in the direction of the next event on the schedule.

Trilock the Magnificent

The evening was settling over the island and the Thuringians sat again in the central room of their suite.

"Trilock the Magnificent," pondered Nestor reflectively. "I daresay the Autharian does deserve this moniker." Each person had in their hand a glass of carbonated lime spritzer. This was bottled, explained their servant, from a spring in the area.

"Great though he may be," observed Artemis, "this does not extend to his chosen competitors. Lemnas won the first prize for knives."

"It was luck," suggested Lemnas modestly.

"I don't believe it and neither do you," responded Artemis keenly.

Lemnas shrugged and smiled. He was pleased with himself and fingered the juniper wreath he had received as mark of his victory.

"You going to the Ceremonial Dance, Nestor?" asked Ajax suddenly.

"Sure I am. Get a chance to see some scantily clad young girls." The others chuckled at old Nestor, and

Nestor laughed along with them.

There came a knock on the door.

"Come!" called out Otzi.

A messenger came forward. "Lord Trilock requests the honor of a meeting with Chief Otzi," he announced.

Otzi raised his eyebrows in surprise. "I am all obedience," he replied, and looked at the others with a bland smile. Then Otzi rose and put on his cloak. He followed the messenger out. The way led in the opposite direction to the Feasting Hall. The shadows of the hall were darkening, and the servants had begun lighting torches against the night. They came at length to a broad doorway. The messenger announced Otzi's arrival.

The room was broad and, in contrast to the others in the lodge, not given over to leisure. It was purposeful, businesslike. There was a broad wooden table in the middle, across which now stretched several marked animal skins. The walls were adorned with woven hangings depicting pictures of animals, trees, and chariots. Trilock nodded in a friendly manner to Otzi. Otzi stepped into the room and came forward. The room was well lit, and windows on one side faced the mountains in the distance. Next to Trilock was Zeras. The right-hand man smiled thinly, which struck Otzi as a bad sign.

"We are just having a look at the maps of our surrounding realms. Please, be welcome. Can I get you anything?" he gestured at the glasses and bottles with various liquids near the wall.

"No, thank you," replied Otzi. He saw now that the animal skins had markings, and that these markings represented the lay of the land thereabouts.

Trilock nodded. "We were just looking at maps of the lands known to us. There are many places of which we have heard, north, south, east and west. We get our information from people like the Ambassador."

"It makes sense," replied Otzi.

"Well, I don't know if you're aware of this, but we've been very active in trade. The salt trade is but one of many ventures. It's an exciting time. I come back to the salt because it's the one thing everyone needs. Gold and rare gems are nice, but you don't die without them. Without salt you may. You can't preserve your goat flank with flecks of silver."

"No indeed," said Otzi.

"The salt mines in the northern regions beyond the mountains have come under our control. This has been a comprehensive effort, a sometimes tiring effort." He chuckled and looked at Zeras. "My headman Zeras here has been instrumental in leading it." Zeras smiled sourly. "He's not such a bad stick, Zeras. Got a bit of a temper, don't you, Zeras? But get a few drinks in him and all's right with the world."

Otzi and Trilock chuckled lightly at Zeras, who stood there motionlessly. "You can help us here, I'm thinking, Otzi. I hope that we can reach some agreement. That is one of the reasons, not the chief one certainly, but one of them, why we invited you and your stout band to this gathering. We need access from our northern mines down here. You control that pass."

"For many generations, yes."

"You are a stout and courageous people. You have done much to control brigandage. Now, however, another system is being put in place, and we will just need your agreement to help it continue."

"I'm not sure I understand," said Otzi, frowning slightly. He knew already what Trilock was getting at. He wanted to play dumb. He wanted to play for time.

Trilock did not hesitate. "The fees you charge for passage across the pass are too high for profitable trade. We want there to be no fees."

"We can discuss the fee, certainly. We're open to adjustments. Particularly if, as you say, you will often be coming over the mountains."

"We will not be paying any fees."

"Then, unfortunately, we will not be allowing your men to pass through our land," replied Otzi, in whose voice was the hardness of cold-forged copper.

"You will not, we think," declared Zeras, "be in a position to resist."

"Letting you through without payment is detrimental to our way of life," declared Otzi flatly.

Zeras spoke now, with a thin smile. "There are many things which are detrimental to a way of life. Death, for example, is detrimental. Torture, to have one's body broken beneath large stones, is detrimental. One's fingers, smashed and twisted, and rendered unusable. One's people, the friends and families of generations, sold into slavery. All these things would be considered by many to be detrimental."

"I appreciate the clarification. We have, as you know, controlled that pass for many, many years. I am not disposed to hand over that control."

"The mighty arm of Trilock is raised, poised to strike," declared Zeras. "Only the mercy which is part of Trilock's lofty character shields you from absolute destruction. Yet still you do not comply!"

Trilock had been looking vaguely into the distance as Zeras said this. "Well, you see, Otzi, it is one of Zeras's unpleasant qualities that he says just what's on his mind.

I don't control these outbursts. Would that I could. And if there is some small grain of truth in them, I still must deplore his manner of delivery."

"Forgive me, this is all very new and surprising," replied Otzi, with an even smile. "I will need time to consider your offer."

"Time is not on your side," shot out Zeras.

"Come, come, Zeras," replied Trilock. "Otzi's time is his own to spend as he wishes. Please, enjoy the evening's festivities."

Otzi nodded and withdrew.

A Hasty Departure

"We need to leave," declared Otzi as he came quickly into the room.

"What's this?" asked Ajax, sitting up in his chair.

"No questions. We've got to go," said Otzi, rushing to collect his possessions. He began jamming them into his backpack.

"How can we?" Artemis stated a basic objection. "We're on an island."

"Need to get clear. Go, go!"

The others leapt up and started collecting their things.

"There's a guard," observed Ajax. Ajax had edged up to the side of the window. He had crept along the wall and was looking out through a slender gap in a curtain. Outside under some trees, fifty yards away, stood five or six Autharian guards. They were looking out at the lake, trying to appear casual. One of them leaned against a tree and looked back at the lodge.

"What can we do?" They looked around urgently. The walls of the lodge were thick stone. There was no budging them. They had to assume that the hallways were guarded.

They would not get away undetected. In one of the rooms they found, in the ceiling, a wooden hatch. Might this lead somewhere?

"We're expected at the dance!" whispered Artemis urgently. "They'll know something is up."

"Quick," said Otzi. They dragged a chair up beneath the hatch. They tested it. With a firm shove it jogged open. Now Ajax climbed up with a boost from Otzi. They found a crawl space. Ajax whispered for them to follow. Carrying their packs on their shoulders, they each of them climbed up.

"We need to hurry," said Ajax, unnecessarily, when they had pulled Nestor up. The crawl space was utterly dark. They followed it for about thirty yards, trying to be as quiet as possible. It made a right-angled turn. After another couple of yards they came across a little foot ladder. They pushed gropingly upward. There was another hatch! This one would not open when they pushed. They felt along the edge and found a hinge. With his knife Otzi slipped into the crack and pulled swiftly down. He pulled against it once. The sound was deafening. They stopped in fright.

Suddenly there were shouts from down below. They could hear people running down the passageway. Otzi imagined at first that he had attracted attention trying to pry free the door. But the alarm only gathered in the distance. Otzi, desperate, jammed down on the hinge a couple more times. The hinge came off. They pushed and pulled and the door came loose. They climbed quickly up. They were on the roof.

The night air greeted them. It was now almost dark and the moon had not yet risen. The cries continued out front. They did not know what the cause was. They could not think. The roof was broad and covered with clay tiles.

Bent down, they ran swiftly along. The far corner of the house was less trafficked than others. Otzi knew, however, that this was none other than Trilock's domain. If either the Lord or Zeras saw them, it would be over. Majestic trees grew on this far side. Around there were no torches; it was dark. They climbed down using the branches of the tree.

Dropping down to the ground, they crouched in the shadows. Unable to resist the temptation, Otzi crept over to peek into the window. Trilock's suite was empty. They listened to the sounds around them.

On the footpath only a few feet from them several guests ran by. "The Chinese Ambassador! Murdered!" One of them cried.

"Great Bel," exclaimed Nestor quietly in horror.

"Now!" cried Otzi and they jumped out of the shadows. They kept to the middle of the island. It was dark and they stumbled along.

"I know!" said Ajax. "The dock." He pulled their sleeves and they followed him. They slid down a leafy dirt hillside, shrouded in darkness. They were near a cut green lawn. They looked out. Nothing so far. Ajax hissed to them to follow. They scampered across to a small dock used by fishermen. For now they had been very fortunate. The night was dark and they could see a fog rolling in over the lake. The boat lacked one thing: oars! Cursing, Ajax jumped out and checked the other boats. In one he found a pair of oars. Meanwhile Otzi untied the boat and they pushed out. Ajax jumped into it and commenced rowing. After a hundred feet or so they unfurled the sail. Although not expert, they managed to get it open and bent to the wind. The boat pushed slowly into the darkness.

"Go south," suggested Nestor.

"Really?" Otzi was doubtful.

"South. There are some marshes at the bottom of the lake. They won't look in that direction. They'll think we hurried straight home."

"It's longer," objected Otzi.

"But not so long as getting caught," insisted Nestor urgently.

"All right." They agreed to travel south down the lake. They would be traveling directly away from their home. The mist was rolling in. Would anyone see them before they got out of sight?

The Death of a Guest

"Calamity! Misfortune!" cried all the guests when they heard the news. "What does it mean?" asked others in dismay. The visitors' rooms were searched, as were those of the islanders and the servants. With many apologies, the guests were summoned to the front of the grounds. When they all were assembled, Zeras looked around.

"The Thuringians. Where are they?" The guests looked around as well. Otzi and his crew were not to be seen.

"They're not here!" cried the guests. "They've fled!"

"My suspicions are confirmed," said Trilock, loud enough for all to hear.

"Otzi fled?" Trilock cried in seeming dismay. "I don't believe it!"

"True, nonetheless, Lord Trilock," replied his second bravely. Zeras had the air of a man whose duty it is to tell unpleasant truths. "I did not want to spoil anyone's entertainment. We've had our suspicions."

"What? What's this?" Trilock turned around sharply.

"Would that I had acted upon it!" Zeras lamented

44

with great regret. "The Chinese Ambassador would still be alive!"

"Let's get hold of yourself, Zeras," advised Trilock sternly. The guests all were following this conversation intently. "We don't know anything. We have a murder. The Thuringians are missing, but that's not the same as guilt. Let them explain, if they can. Find them."

The guests, although they appreciated Trilock's sense of fairness, believed overwhelmingly in the guilt of the mountain men. Or else why were they not here?

Lorran and the members of his contingent looked at each other, saying nothing. They did speak openly, lest they too become suspect of the crime. When they were alone, they made plans to get away quickly. They did not believe in the guilt of Otzi and his friends.

"If they are guilty, let judgment be visited upon them," Trilock was saying again. "In the meantime, let search parties be formed. But oh! I have lost a friend. Lao-Tse!" Lord Trilock's shoulders shook with grief, and his servants had to help lead him away.

"We will see to this, sir," called Zeras after him in a reassuring voice. "Come, men of arms!" he nodded to his men. "Quickly. We must comply with Lord Trilock's wishes."

They rushed off to start the preparations.

Hill and Dale

"Trilock the Magnificent," Artemis repeated as she and the others trudged through the soupy swampland south of Lake Donoma. The boat had taken them south. The waters had been very still overnight, and around them the fog had been thick. A gentle lapping against the hull and the dipping of oars had been the only sounds. The light returned slowly. A gray desolation was all about them. The boat edged forward into the morning. Rushes gathered in islands and prevented their further progress. They backtracked with the oars and found their way into the main stream. The occasional cry of a marsh bird punctuated the growing brightness of the day.

When they could go no farther, they jumped out and sank to their chests. They trudged forward, wading in places. The boat they dragged with them until at last they came to something resembling dry land. It was still early. They were far away from Autharia Island, but farther also from their destination. They needed a breather and something to eat. They found a clump which was higher than the rest. Above them was a cluster of ash trees. They kindled a small fire and dried their clothes. With them were some dried fruits and ibex which they'd brought with them.

"Salted meat," commented Lemnas with a wry smile.

"Trilock was magnificent at getting us into trouble," commented Ajax, shaking his head.

"I blame myself," said Otzi. "And I apologize to the rest of you. We should never have accepted their invitation."

"There is no blame at all," said Ajax. "We followed the dictates of Perchta."

"We might have paid similar respect to Perchta simply by going to our neighboring village."

"This trouble would have come upon us anyway. As your man said"—Nestor meant Trilock. Already it was distasteful to him to speak the Autharian leader's name out loud— "the Thuringian Pass is strategic. They would have attacked us in due time."

"But now we have let down our people. They will face attack unprepared."

"Give them some credit, Tribal Chief. They're vigilant, particularly in our absence," reassured him Ajax.

"Hmm." Otzi did not need to say that it would likely not be enough. The village of the Thuringians numbered two hundred or more strong. Of these there were perhaps seventy-five strong warriors. The assembled forces of Trilock and his allies could offer three or four times that number. If, in addition, they acted without warning, their advantage would be greater."

Otzi shook his head, saying nothing. The fire crackled as the morning crept along. It was very worrying to think about. Artemis looked gravely out over the marshland.

"What do we do now?" asked Ajax.

"We go east as fast as possible. We can't take the same

routes. We have to assume that Zeras and his men are following us. They will watch all the usual roads. We need to take unknown paths. It will be difficult."

"Our absence makes us look guilty," pointed out Ajax.

"Our presence would have made us look dead," countered Otzi.

"They will come after us."

"Yes," replied Otzi stolidly.

"Now more than ever do we need the assistance of Perchta," Ajax sighed and got ready to continue.

The Pursuit

Soon the travelers were on their way again. They walked to the edge of the swamp. The ground rose. They were in a canyon which went north and south, judging from the sun. They needed to go east. To go in that direction, they would have to go up, climbing the steep hillside.

With swift and purposeful steps the group began to walk uphill. The day was becoming warm and the woods grew thickly over the lower reaches of the hill. When they had gotten past the lower reaches, they found a path which led upward. The way offered barely room for them to walk. Probably it was just an animal track. The way was not steep at first, but then it began to double back upon itself to make the climb.

They paused for water. "A hot one," commented Nestor.

"It is," replied Artemis.

After several hours the trees began to thin out. They came into a broad meadow. Then came a troubling sound: a howl. Animals were in the neighborhood. Not just any animals—wolves. By the sound of it there were many of them. After a moment an answering cry could be heard on the other side of them.

Zeras had spent the foregoing hours organizing search parties. They had levied men from all the villages of Autharia. These men stood on the shore of the lake, ready to get going. Zeras gave each group its instructions. The groups comprised twelve to fifteen men. The men in each group gave a shout. With promise of reward they moved out quickly. Now Zeras spoke to the horsemen. He had separated these into three groups of ten. The horses had been imported from the steppes in the east, or what would eventually be called the Ukraine. The horsemen could cover a lot of ground. Zeras would lead one of these equestrian contingents. With a shout to the others he gave the order to set forth.

"We may face a danger besides just Trilock," observed Otzi drily. They continued to climb. They heard, now and again, more howls. It was hard to tell in the breeze of the mountain but they appeared to be coming closer. A grassy upland stretched out before them. At the distance of about a mile was a ridge. They needed to make for the ridge.

They saw a wolf, marked gray against the green grass. It was coming toward them. "We're expecting visitors!" said Ajax, and he drew his sword. Soon they saw a number of wolves tearing across the opposite hill toward them. Otzi looked about him.

"We need to expect them from all angles!" he cried.

They all drew their weapons. Ajax pointed to something in the distance. Otzi nodded and started looking about them. "Quick, that log!" he said with a shout. The crew ran swiftly to an old fallen log. They began to drag the log in the direction they were tending. The wolves pulled up short at a distance of a hundred feet away. They looked appraisingly at the humans.

"It's going to get hot in a minute!" said Otzi, helping to drag the log. The wolf's ears were pinned back and he began to snarl. Otzi lifted his blade to the threat. It was a medium-sized blade, broad rather than long. It was good for hacking, and it was sharp enough to cut a human hair.

Now six or seven wolves fanned out. Howls could be heard from other directions. How many of them were there? Lemnas fingered his knives as he considered the battle ahead. The youth felt confident about getting off one or two knives. Hand-to-hand combat with an adult wolf would be a tricky maneuver, however.

Now there came a snarl from behind them. They wheeled around. Artemis did not hesitate. She aimed a shaft at the wolf behind them. It hit the wolf in the shoulder, a damaging but not mortal blow. The wolf limped back out of the fray. Artemis also had a short sword, which she could use in such situations as these.

"They will all attack at once," said Otzi. "Form a circle facing out!" Just then the lead wolf sprang forward. Artemis drew and released. The arrow passed through the stomach of the wolf and it fell down in a heap. The others now leapt forward as well. The Thuringians knew much of wolves from their home. They knew that quick lateral movements might fool large wolves, who carried with them a lot of heft. They shifted quickly now and stabbed at the oncoming wolves.

A very large wolf fell below Otzi's blade, but the sword got stuck. Another wolf came for Otzi. Nestor jabbed at this one with his staff, putting off the wolf, who careered off to the side. Otzi pulled out a knife and was ready for the next wolf. This wolf snapped at the head Thuringian, catching at the hem of his garment. Otzi jabbed quickly with his knife at the wolf's shoulder blade, and the wolf sprang away with a yelp.

Artemis had fired off half a dozen arrows, and they all had found a target. Lemnas also had been true. A knife lay buried in the throat of a fallen wolf. The wolves were undaunted by the response. Ajax was fearsome with his large blade. He stepped forward, hacking at two wolves who came close enough. Again the wolves yelped and snarled, then pulled back. "Perchta, guide me!" shouted out Ajax, who wheeled around to see if others were coming. He shouted ferociously at the wolves. Whether because of his fierce appearance or because of the mention of Perchta, the wolves hesitated. In that moment, Otzi began frantically to pull at the log. They had to move it before the wolves recovered the initiative.

"Come, help me!" he shouted to the others. The others came up to the log and helped to drag it along. They stopped before something they had seen. It was a narrow crevasse, perhaps twenty feet wide. With an effort they lifted the tree upright. It was now standing a couple of feet back from the edge. They let it drop down across the crevasse. The tree was long enough to reach the other side by a few feet. They pushed it a little forward.

"Here we cross," declared Otzi. Lemnas, light and dexterous, skipped across to the other side. Next came Artemis. She did it also, with not too much difficulty. The group had a short length of rope, perhaps fifteen feet in length. Nestor and Ajax attached the rope each to the other. They walked across. If one slipped, the other would tumble down the other side. The rope would loop them over the log, and they could scramble up again. So went the theory, at least.

The wolves had recovered their purpose. They approached to within twenty feet of where Otzi was standing. He held his sword to safeguard Nestor and Ajax. The two walked carefully across the wooden bridge.

"You need to hurry," Otzi said through gritted teeth. They had made it. A snarling wolf came charging at Otzi. He dashed to one side and thrust at the wolf as it passed. The wolf yelped at the slash and ran to a safe distance again.

"The rope!" called back Otzi while the others watched from across the gap. Ajax threw the coil across. It almost didn't make it across. It would have slid down into the depths, but it caught on a snag of the log. "Nice," said Otzi sarcastically. He was looking for a branch to which he could tie the rope. Then, if he fell, he could throw the branch across in hopes of stopping himself.

Then the wolves attacked again. Otzi, without thinking, jumped up on the log and darted across it. He was sure that a wolf was behind him. The wolf was smarter than they were. It looked at the log. It put its foot on the log. Then it pulled the foot back. The distance across was too great to jump. The distance down was too deep to survive. The wolves snarled at them angrily from the other side of the crevasse.

The humans dislodged the log, sending it dropping down into the depths. They walked along, laughing with relief.

Messengers Are Sent

Trilock sat at a table in the enclosed courtyard outside his suite. He was writing brief notes of instruction upon carefully cut pieces of birch bark. The marks he made upon the bark were simple etched lines. These would be understood by the person to whom he was sending them. On the table was a wire containing a wooden cage containing a dozen or so pigeons. The wooden slats were too narrow for the birds to slip through. Next to the cage was a servant. At a nod from Trilock the servant opened the cage and removed one bird. He brought the bird to the Autharian Lord. Trilock attached the rolled-up bark with a string to the talon of the bird. He released the pigeon with a brief upward thrust of his hands. The pigeon would deliver the message to a faraway place.

Sincha of Leponto lay on a reclining chair in the sun of the courtyard. She wore a robe which lay open to the sun. She made no movement and said nothing. Her stillness acted as a reproach to the Lord of the Island.

"You are upset with these methods?" he asked her, writing on another piece of bark.

Sincha said nothing.

"You are sorry that the man, Otzi, had to be chosen?"

"No," Sincha said tonelessly.

"It is not the man but the place. We must act as best suits the interests of Autharia."

"Yes," she said, still with no expression in her voice.

Trilock said nothing more. He nodded to the servant, who brought another bird, With a sudden ferocious wrench Trilock twisted the neck of the bird. It did not move after that.

Sincha gasped. Trilock looked over at her with a bland smile. "In time, you will come to understand the wisdom of all my decisions," said he.

The Rustic Cottage

The afternoon was getting on as the travelers walked down the far side of the mountain. They were tired from the day's hike and said little to each other. Otzi was thinking of the journey they had undertaken. Now they would have to engage in a perilous return trip. All of this had been undertaken out of curiosity! Why had they not simply gone to the local Kula as necessary? They would not be in peril, and the village would not be in peril.

Otzi's wife, Ana, had foreseen this clearly enough. "Why does he invite you?" she had asked when the smiling messenger departed their town.

Otzi, she, and their young boy sat in the main room of their house on the slope overlooking Thurin Town. The spring had been lovely. The snows had melted early from a week of unbroken sunshine. A stream ran through the middle of Thurin Valley. The musical fall of fast-rushing waters could be heard in the distance.

"I don't know," Otzi replied, more amused than anything else. Ana was a strong woman, rather stout and maternal. Her light brown hair was pulled back from her face as she performed chores around the cottage. "The name of Thuringia is becoming known far and wide," offered Otzi with a smile.

"Thurin Village has prospered under your leadership, it is true," replied Ana evenly. "This in itself should make us cautious." Otzi had known Ana since they were children. When he was younger, Otzi had been too wild to settle down. He had gotten into all sorts of adventures. But even when he was doing this, he had said to himself that Ana would be the girl he would marry. They had a young son, Gula, who played on the reed carpet. He promised to be a strapping lad. He was but four but was bigger than the other boys of his age.

Ana looked at him with her clear gray eyes and said nothing. She knew him better than he knew himself, he reflected. She had known that Otzi, once he'd made up his mind to accept the invitation, would not change it. Now Otzi bitterly regretted that he had not listened to her words of caution.

On the other hand, they knew the danger now. Getting out in the world had helped them to see it from farther off. Trilock had lured him out of safety. If the Autharian ruler had succeeded in killing him or at least getting him out of the way, the village would have been in trouble. The village still was in trouble. However, if by some small chance Otzi and his team managed to wind through to the mountains again, they would be on guard against future danger. Perhaps, then, the journey would not be such a loss. The chance was small, as he well knew.

Otzi began to think of strategies for their survival. There was one option, perhaps. But no, it was too much of a long shot even to consider! He tried to push it from his mind.

The sun was low on the horizon when the group came

again into the flatland. The land here was grassy and uncultivated. The ground here was damp from a spring somewhere nearby. They looked over the plain which lay before them. The land sloped ever-so-slightly downhill for several miles. In the distance about a mile away they saw a hut. They needed now to get some information. They walked in the direction of the hut.

A garrison of fighting men sat in a camp in the high foothills beneath the Alps Mountains. The air was cool and the forest dark and piney here. The winds swept mournfully through the treeline. The captain was a worn-faced veteran of many wars. His hair was dusted with gray and his face slashed across his cheek. He was a brawny man, with his face cast in a perpetual frown. He looked down through the valley they'd come up a couple of weeks before. They expected to get word to move any day now. Their supplies of food were running low. The land here was flat before it stepped upward again toward the heights. Across this staging area were dotted thirty or more tents. In these were resting veterans personally approved by their leader.

There was a flicker and a flutter, and the great bird appeared on a tree stump. It made no movement. It waited calmly, as it had been trained to do. The leader went to the camp table and scraped off a few shreds of meat from the meal before. He brought these as a gift for the falcon. The bird made no movement at the man approached. He reached for its talon. Attached to this was a message. There were no words, merely a symbol. *Well, all right.* thought the man. He handed the scraps to the hawk and the bird, after taking these, stepped onto his hand. He pushed upward and the bird once more took flight.

One of the warriors came up to him. "What's the word from Authoria?" asked the man boldly.

"We start right away," said the leader.

"What, tonight?"

"Yes. Get the men ready," He turned to the other with a stern glance.

"Yes, sir," replied the fighting man, who rushed off to carry out this order.

The visitors approached the small rustic hut. The sun now was no more than an orange stain against the mountains in the west. As they drew near, they saw a man seated on a bench outside the hut. He was playing a lyre. He had to have noticed the strangers' approach yet he made no sign. Seemingly immersed in the music, he continued to play his soulful tune.

When he finished, the visitors murmured their approval. The man nodded to them in welcome. He was elderly, with gray cropped hair and a creased, clean-shaven face. The hut was humble of construction. He sat on a porch, and stretching out before him was a vegetable garden and trickle at the bottom of it. "Welcome, travelers," said he. "I knew of your coming a couple of hours ago."

"You knew?" asked Ajax, surprised.

"The wolves inform me of strangers' approach. They patrol the westward hills the year round. If travelers be hardy and courageous, they come eventually to my door."

"If not they come to a wolf's belly, is that it?" laughed Otzi.

"Just so," replied the man, chuckling. "I am Naithair," said he. "My family is not far away. They will bring food for dinner soon. If you are hungry, please join me. If you are weary, please rest the night here."

"Thank you for your offer, sir," replied the foremost Thuringian. "I am Otzi, and these friends of mine and I are traveling east. We come from over the mountains yonder." He pointed back westward, where, in the far distance, a line of white peaks loomed.

"The road is long," said the man simply. "Rest, clean up. Later, if you wish, you will tell me of your journey." The old man climbed to his feet and beckoned toward the open door. The hut was modestly sized but it was clean. Either Naithair or one of his family saw to the upkeep of the place. Naithair went down into the garden. Two young girls, maybe eleven and thirteen, made their way up a path to him. Naithair picked up a pail. One girl took it and walked down the path. She returned with a full pail of water. The other girl carried a basket. She handed it to the old man. The girls looked with shy curiosity at the travelers. Then they turned again down the path. Out front was a fire pit. Nestor began kindling a fire into life.

The night fell and the fire licked up toward the cloudy sky. The visitors and the old man sat about the fire. Their plates were empty for they had finished a meal of braised goat and salad. They were feeling peaceful. The travelers did not feel very urgently the pursuit of Zeras. He and his concerns seemed very far from this place. The land about here was lonely and quiet.

The man's daughter had joined them and listened

to the talk. She watched the glowing logs. A neighbor also had joined them, a gaunt, dark man named Troilus. Troilus took the lyre and began to play on it. Ajax felt a sense of well-being around these simple folks. He had wanted to attend the Kula. His reverence for Perchta, the Moon Goddess, had made this an essential undertaking. Autharia had seemed too fancy to him. He had matched fists with the Autharians. Apart from that, he had not felt very comfortable.

"Do you get many visitors?" asked Ajax. "I mean, of those who make it past the wolves."

"Not many, no. We get some to whom I am not so friendly. You say you come from the east?"

"From over those mountains, yes," Ajax gestured.

"Strange folk come from beyond the white mountains." He gestured at white peaks in the far distance. "I do not well understand them. They are different."

"Do they speak our language?"

"One can make them out. But they have strange customs. They worship different gods." Naithir shook his head.

"Perchta, the Moon Goddess, they must worship."

"I don't know," replied Naithir.

"But they must!" rejoined Ajax with warmth. "She is the moon."

"Perhaps the moon does not visit those parts," replied Naithair thoughtfully.

Ajax frowned and said nothing. "Even if she does not show them her face, she is there."

"I agree," said the woman, daughter of Naithair. She smiled reassuringly at Ajax. He broke into a rueful grin.

"I get worked up." He shrugged. She nodded.

The man with the lyre, Troilus, began to sing. He

had a sweet, high tenor voice and seemed to know many songs. Old Nestor fell into a reverie. He recalled his earlier days. Tears came to his eyes as he thought back on former times. Naithair passed around a gourd of fermented black-currant wine. Soon everybody was feeling warm and calm.

Otzi prompted Naithair about the local area. Naithair explained that he had come here from the eastern seacoast many years ago. He had been seeking to escape a war which was then raging. Once out here, he was left alone for the most part. He started a family. People did not favor this region because the soil was poor. Most of the business around here was in raising livestock.

"Can you tell me, then, Naithair," inquired Otzi in a casual voice, "which way is best going east from here?"

"Depends how you want to do it," replied Naithair.

"We'd just as soon not attract much attention," replied Otzi and held his breath. Were these the sorts of people to give them away?

Naithair did not seem surprised or shocked.

"We don't know the people in these parts," added Otzi, to soften the meaning of his words. "We know you, of course, and it's nice to meet you."

"It's a quiet part of the country. It is the back of beyond," he replied with a smile. "We have some characters, though."

"Hmm, yes," replied Otzi with an answering smile.

"Now we have this big man running things. 'Lord' Trilock, as he calls himself." The old man shook his head ruefully. "I don't remember giving him authority over me. People like that want something, I don't raise my hand. It's going to come back to bite you eventually."

"You're right," said Otzi.

"They can join the cattle drive," said Naithair's

daughter suddenly. "Don't take this the wrong way, but perhaps you'd just as soon not attract attention."

"No offense taken," answered Ajax.

"People coming from the west often are in some kind of spot." She was a small, dark woman, direct in her way of speaking. It was nice to have an ally, thought Otzi. Evidently his daughter shared Naithair's distrust of the authorities.

"Hmm, yes," considered Naithair. "That's a good idea."

"Cattle drive?" asked Ajax.

"They take the cattle down to pastures in the lowland," explained the daughter. "They'll take you on. Here—" she broke off and got up. She disappeared down the path.

"It started yesterday. This will help you stay low to the ground," observed Naithair. "We thank you from the bottom of our hearts," said Otzi with feeling.

"You'd do the same for me in a pinch. Not that I plan on going anywhere anytime soon."

Troilus continued to strum softly on the lyre.

"Is it hard, driving cattle?" asked Ajax. There weren't too many cattle in the mountains. A few yaks maybe.

"You can pick it up in a couple hours," said Naithair. "About five miles south of here."

"Oh is it?" Ajax nodded.

"They'll be looking to take on people. You'll need different clothes though."

"Your daughter is a fine woman!" declared Nestor admiringly.

"Yes, she's had a hard life. When her husband died, she was left to contend with everything that came up."

"Difficult indeed. Yet admirable," replied Otzi. The daughter came back. She was carrying a bundle of clothes.

She seemed to sense that the men had been talking about her. She smiled, slyly and demurely, which added much liveliness to her face.

"You can't stand out," she explained. "Too warm for fur animal-skin cloaks around here."

"We're from the mountains," explained Nestor.

"Well, put these on." She handed them some loose-fitting cotton shirts and broad-brimmed sun hats. The hats would conceal the visitors' features. Naithair rose to indicate that he was tired. The visitors, who had to get up early, rose too.

Amongst the Ranchers

The visitors woke early and got ready to leave. Naithair was already up. They drank some tea and set off, thanking him heartily. In the distance the woman with her daughters and son waved to them. They followed the river as instructed by Naithair. With them was the thin-faced neighbor who had sung so beautifully the night before.

The land fell away. They were going downhill. The trickle now had gathered into a narrow stream. It gurgled beside them as they walked. They approached a cluster of huts which stood about this stream. They were low, broad, and circular. The roofs were covered in thick, bristly thatching.

Beyond the huts was a large area set off by a wooden fence. Cattle milled around this area. Children and family members could be seen walking between some huts. Others served the business of cattle herding. The foremost hut had a porch, and on this stood several men looking out on the morning. These men were solidly built and weathered. Their hands were calloused and they wore brimmed hats to shelter them from the hot sun. Naithair's neighbor Troilus approached the man rather hesitantly. Otzi and the group stood at a distance. They could hear Troilus talking to them and gesturing toward them. A large, strong-looking man looked over and beckoned to the Thuringians. Otzi and Ajax approached.

The man looked them up and down frankly and offered a word in greeting.

"Greetings, sir," replied Otzi, with modest dignity.

"I'm hearing you'd like to drive cattle."

"We would, yes, please," replied the mountaineer.

"You been around cattle before?" asked the man.

"Yes indeed. Often," replied Otzi.

The man nodded with amusement. All workers say that, Otzi knew. "We can't pay you much," said the man.

"Not much is better than nothing," replied Otzi with a workingman's stoicism. They did not need money; they had brought enough with them. But Otzi did not want to invite suspicion by offering to work for no pay. The man nodded, still smiling knowingly. Otzi would have been surprised to learn that many of these rough-and-ready types had come over those westward hills over the years. Being a ranch hand was hard work. The good part was that people didn't ask nosy questions. "Ten minutes," said Gooch finally. "What do we call you?"

"This is Ajax, and I am Otzi."

"Gooch," said the big man.

"Gooch is the big boss," put in one of the rancher's men sitting on the porch.

Gooch nodded distantly, as befits an employer. Otzi and Ajax retreated. He was willing to take them on, they considered, and that was the main thing.

Otzi returned to the others. They went down to the stream to fill their skins before the day began.

Zeras and his assembled henchmen galloped east across the flat and fertile plain. The horses were still an unusual sight to people in those parts. Thundering down the roads in the early morning, Zeras and his men caused consternation in the local folk. Zeras lamented these developments, although such things, in his experience, did happen. It had not been part of the plan to allow Otzi to escape the island. Incriminating clues had been collected from the Thuringians' gear while they were away at dinner. These had been planted in the rooms of the Chinese Ambassador. Trilock could not resist the dramatic meeting with Otzi. Obviously the meeting had spooked the mountain man, who had acted quickly. He and his friends had shown ingenuity to escape. The only positive was that with their hasty departure, guilt had not been difficult to allege. The other guests had reacted with revulsion to the crime and urged action against the mountain folk. If some had suspected another explanation for the events, they had not spoken aloud.

Now, however, Trilock and Zeras needed to tie up the loose ends. They needed to kill Otzi. Already the armed contingent was going to take control of the Thuringian Pass. With Otzi out of the way and judged to have been the killer, no one would object too strongly to Trilock's muscular course of action.

But where were the mountaineers? They had survival skills, and Otzi was a tricky character. But the flatlands were well patrolled and easy to search. Zeras knew that Otzi would try to get home as quickly as possible. He had opted not to take the direct route, a sign of intelligence. He was now on some side path, some animal track, making his capture difficult. But they would catch them, Zeras knew. This was the sort of thing the head of Autharian security excelled at.

Zeras's horse was like her master: haughty, imperious, and willful. Zeras had grown up in these parts. His family had enjoyed some standing until the untimely death of his father. Instead of accepting their diminished position, Zeras boarded a ship for war-torn lands. There he hired himself out as a mercenary, then as a commander, and finally as a tactician. Although still a young man, Zeras had earned a reputation for effectiveness. In the event of an attack upon a rival city, a raid upon a convoy, or suppression of local people, Zeras got the job done. For this he demanded, and received, a high fee.

One day, just as he was beginning to grow tired of the soldiering life, a messenger appeared. This man claimed to represent Lord Trilock of Autharia. Zeras recalled this name from his youth. Trilock's father had been a force in the area of what's now called northern Italy. Trilock the son had added lands on his own account. He had also added the epithet "The Magnificent." Zeras did not respect Trilock. He did not like people with big mouths. However, he did respect the compensation which was offered for his services. Zeras's job was to make sure Trilock's lofty pronouncements ended in concrete results. Zeras agreed to become Trilock's right-hand man.

This situation, however, was critical. The local chiefs would not have bought the story of Otzi's guilt. They would only believe it once the head of Otzi was presented to them on a stake. Anything less than this, and suddenly Trilock would look a little less magnificent.

Zeras's horse surged down the road in the morning light. She was a swift, high-shouldered beast capable of great speed. Now horse and rider galloped across the plains in search of some highly inconsiderate houseguests.

The Rustlers Attack

The drive consisted of several hundred head of cattle. The stock was strong and well nourished, beefy animals with glossy brown and white hides. Before them in the line trotted the calves. The little ones ambled proudly in front of their slow-moving parents. The late-summer heat was upon the land. The track was broad and dusty. The dirt was of a whitish color, covering the travelers from head to foot. Gooch rode to one side of the train on a solid, heavy-footed horse. The herders walked along with the livestock. They carried little switches with which they slapped the animals from time to time. Herding dogs helped to keep the animals from running off on a tangent. Whenever a number of animals made a break, the dogs would block them, snapping at their legs. By these nips and snarls they would succeed in leading most of the cattle back to the line.

The Thuringians walked along with the moving train. It was a tiring business requiring constant attention. The dust and the heat of the day began to tell on them. They rested for a short time sometime after midday and Gooch motioned them over take some food. Bread and cheese was offered and a surprisingly nice wheat drink. Gooch did not talk to them, merely looking silently over the shimmering plain. He sat at a distance and exchanged occasional two-word sallies with a subordinate.

There were twelve or fifteen other hands along on the drive. After half an hour the drive resumed. Otzi looked at Ajax and they shared a grin. Two days ago they had been dining on the finest delicacies of the region. Now they were marching beside dull animals for grub and a few coppers a day.

Somewhere to the south away a mile or two hence was the great Heckla River. In modern times this broad band of water would be called the Po. Nestor told them of these parts, for he had been here many years before. The land was parched from days of sun and no rain. Farmland stretched out to either side. In the distance the farmhands could be seen swinging their scythes. The track was almost a half-mile wide, barren and winding to accommodate planted fields. The hooves marched along in a patient line.

Ajax had been concerned about the group's weapons. Carrying them along with them, he felt, would make them too conspicuous. He was afraid that Zeras's people would be around any minute to check on the drive. Ajax noticed that some of the cattle were saddled to be ridden by the smaller ranch hands. A couple of these lads rode cows, who bore their weight with no difficulty. Ajax had managed to attach the group's weapons to one of the empty saddles. He did not lose sight of this cow. Their weapons might be needed at any time.

After several hours Gooch rode up beside Otzi. "You say you come from out west?"

"Yes," replied the tribal chief warily. "From over the mountains."

"You have any trouble getting over?" asked Gooch.

"Just the usual," replied Otzi, making a joke of it. "Wolves, brigands, drought, and mosquitos."

"That's about right," replied Gooch, and he moved off again. The day grew cloudy in the afternoon and there was a growing heaviness to the air. It looked like they might have a thunderstorm. Across the horizon big, stacked clouds formed. In the distance they could see sheets of rain settling down over the fields. Beams of light shone through these gray curtains of wetness.

They expected to hear a mighty clap of thunder. Instead they heard the fearful shout of one of the ranch hands. Otzi looked around. They saw a half-dozen men on horses bearing down on them at speed!

Ajax ran quickly to the weapons cache. He pulled them off the riderless cow's saddle. The other hands held up the long sticks they used for herding. These would serve as weapons. They were being attacked by rustlers.

Gooch pulled from his saddle a heavy club. His slow horse patrolled back and forth across one flank in an attempt to block the thieves' path. The rustlers stayed out of range. They did not intend a direct attack. Instead they galloped around the back and the front of the lines, shouting and waving their weapons. One of them, midcry, fell silent and reached for his throat. One of Artemis's arrows had found it. Before his soul quite had time to begin its journey to the afterlife, Otzi was after the horse. The man swayed in the saddle and Otzi grabbed one of the reins. He pulled down the man and jumped up into the saddle himself. The horse panicked and galloped off across a field. The dead man was trampled by a hundred heavy hooves.

The rustlers' efforts were having an effect. The cattle

began to stampede. Otzi meanwhile was struggling to control the horse. He was being pulled away from the line. One of the rustlers saw a cluster of cattle lagging off to one side. He tried to lead them away from the main group. While concentrating on this plan, he did not see his danger. Ajax made a running leap onto the back of a cow. The cow began to run in the direction of the rustler. When it was close enough Ajax leapt again. Ajax tackled the man off his horse. Winded, the man could not move. Ajax smashed his face in a moment with a rock. Ajax ran to catch up with the man's horse. The horse kept just out of his grasp. The bridle jingled in the moist late-afternoon air.

The Protection of a Goddess

The search for the stray cattle continued an hour later. Gooch had managed to pull most of the herd together. The hands worked hard to keep them in line. The rustlers had been driven off. Gooch did not seem much surprised by the incident. He claimed even to know the father of one of the dead thieves. Gooch clapped young Lemnas on the back and promised him double rations that evening. Lemnas grinned with pleasure at the big boss's praise.

The fields were high with swaying gray-yellow wheat. Ajax found himself on a lonely path some distance from the drive. The lane was rutted from wagon traffic. He had seen a few head of cattle rove off in this direction. He was determined to find them before evening settled in. Ajax heard the rumble of several horses down the lane. There was nowhere to hide.

The horses pulled up to the solitary mountain man. These were Zeras's men. The chief rider approached Ajax, who turned his horse around to meet him. The man had his hand upon the hilt of his sword. Ajax would not prevail in any clash of arms.

"You are part of a cattle train?"

"That is correct, sir," replied Ajax respectfully.

"Where are you from?"

"We are from behind the mountains yonder," Ajax replied, pointing to the west. "We saw an opportunity to earn a few meals to help us with our travels."

"We are looking for some strangers. One of them fits your description."

"I would say that he fits my description only distantly," replied Ajax, keeping his voice low.

"It is true that, in some respects, there is a similarity," observed the rider. His tone seemed to suggest that he was talking to himself. "But after all the likeness is not so great."

"We are looking simply to continue our travels," said Ajax in the same undertone.

"You should be allowed to continue your travels," put in the rider.

The man, having reached this point, seemed at a loss as to how to proceed. There came a shout from behind him. Another rider came charging up. "Got something!" he cried.

"Coming," said the man. He nodded amiably at Ajax before turning his horse around and galloping off.

"The Moon Goddess, Perchta, favors us," said Ajax softly as he watched the men go.

Lemnas and Nestor were walking down a path between a windbreak and a harvested field. Lemnas had seen a couple of calves march off in this direction. He had with him a rope by which hoped to slow the calves. With them also was a herding dog. The dog ran excitedly ahead of them. The calves were found peacefully tearing leaves off the lower branches of some alder trees. The dog nipped them and the calves turned reluctantly back up the road. Nestor and Lemnas followed behind.

Nestor looked slyly over at the boy. "What?" said Lemnas.

"You have been attracting a certain favorable notice of late, old son," observed Nestor.

"What?" Lemnas protested, blushing.

"These lowland girls seem to have it in for you."

"I have no idea what you're talking about!" cried Lemnas.

Nestor smiled benevolently. Lemnas felt irritated. "Some years ago," he began, "I don't care to say how many—a lot. Very many. I was down in these parts before."

"Do I want to hear this?" Lemnas asked nervously.

"There was a girl, fair to look upon and oh so young. Her father was a farmer, a worthy man still in the prime of his years."

"Okay?" Lemnas frowned, eager for this story to come to an end.

"I asked that girl for her hand in marriage. The father agreed that she should become my first wife."

"But not your second?" Lemnas quipped with a sidelong glance. Nestor had made several marriages. Thurin's gallant Troubadour chose to ignore the aside.

"That girl is Telya now," Nestor began suggestively.

"I still don't know what in Orcus you mean."

"Fine, fine." Lemnas found his elder's indulgent smile very irritating. Nestor winked at him. "It will be our little secret, as between men."

Lemnas knew, of course, what Nestor was talking

about. He preferred not to discuss it. But when they returned to the line he caught the smoldering glances of the aforementioned Telya cast in his direction.

Two broad fields of the lowlands stretched out on all sides. In the middle of this was an intersection of two roads. Two farmers approached this crossing. One came from the south, and the other from the west. They rolled along in wagons which were pulled by oxen. They nodded to each other as they met in the crossing. One cart pulled up alongside the other.

"Well, Dallus, how's doings in your parts?" one asked.

"Hmm, you know how it is, Dael. Been working to get the crop all in."

"Take your time!" replied the other. "We harvested a couple of weeks ago."

"Conditions are different over here."

"Are you almost through?"

The other shrugged as if to say, "We'll be through when we're through." They looked over the familiar fields. Both men had lived in the district their whole lives. "Say, ain't this a thing about them mountain folks?"

The other farmer shook his head with mournful relish. "Now they done gone and killed the Ambassador of China. Over there by Lord Trilock's Kula."

"That was stupid."

"These mountain folks are crazy," said the other. The men were about the same age, in their fifties, with shorn, choppy haircuts and round, well-fed faces.

"Managed to get off Autharian Island without getting caught up. Now he and his bunch has lit out. They say this

Otzi must be some boy."

"Resourceful."

"You're right, Dael. Mind you, now we have Lord Trilock's men gone after them." "They'll get it done." The other farmer nodded vaguely. He looked out over the fields. "You'll see. Trilock's got some rough boys of his own."

The other farmer nodded. "You're right. It don't pay to go up against Lord Trilock."

The other looked over at his longtime friend. "You know what I heard? Kianha has been asking after you."

"That would be your wife?"

"She is? Don't tell none of them other girls!"

"What did Kianha say?"

"Something about that Dallus, why he don't come over and get some apple pie?" "Well, shoot, if that's how she feels about it," replied his neighbor.

"Just don't come over when I'm not around," replied the other with a grin, and tipped his hat. The farmers nodded and went their separate ways.

The Watering Hole

The ranchers came in the evening to a broad watering hole. The large pond had formed in a dip in the land. Water was fed by a stream and perhaps a spring in the area. The water was surprisingly fresh. The excited cattle splashed down into it and remained there, half-sunk in the waves. They were done for the day, they seemed to be telling the humans.

As it happened this was the ranchers' plan. The ranch hands settled down into little camps. An hour after Gooch's drive arrived another drive came up. Gooch now had to work to keep his cattle separate from the newcomers'. A couple of ranch hands brought over fresh food for Otzi and the others. This had been transported in a wagon that they'd brought with them. Otzi and the others looked forward to a hearty meal. "Lemnas!" Artemis called out to attract the attention of the mountain youth.

Lemnas had been enjoying the adventure. He did not quite understand the disagreement between his tribe's chief, Otzi, and the Autharian chief, Trilock. He knew about the salt trade and about disagreements. The moves and countermoves he had been able to grasp intellectually. He could not as yet understand the passions which lay behind these actions. The world of adults was full of violent likes and dislikes, reflected the young Lemnas. He felt himself apart from it still.

All that he had seen and experienced had been, for him, wonderful. The journey had been his first to the flatlands. He found the warm, soupy summer air exciting. It awakened in him snatches of a dream. Lemnas's seventeen years had been spent in the mountains and foothills. He had dreams, however, of much more than this!

Travelers came through the village and brought with them stories of far-off places. The broad seas were, to hear these people talk, packed with navies and pirates who preyed upon shipping. Life depended in large part upon the swiftness of one's blade. Lemnas had been pleased to come in first in the knife-throwing competition. Through constant practice he had become good at this skill. He did not doubt but that he would have to dispatch a few enemies before the trip was over. Things were shaping up that way. He did not trouble himself much over the prospect of taking another's life. Adventures invariably were bloody affairs, and the death of others was a part of it. In any case, that person's ultimate fate depended not on Lemnas. It depended on the infinitely wise decisions of Perchta, the Moon Goddess and Bel, God of the Sun. Departed souls did not die. They simply stepped out of the adventure.

The Fascination of Women

But women, now that was something of which to be fearful! The girls in his native village were clean-limbed and athletic. They were, generally, unemotional. They looked daily upon the ice-bound peaks around them. These mountains, cold and sharply cut, were unforgiving: a storm might blow in upon them, and the mountain drop a hundred yards of snow upon some mere wanderer's head. They could be sunny too. These were the emotions which Lemnas felt instinctively to be his. He wanted to be cold, like the mountain, to be fierce, to be sudden. The girls of the lowlands were different creatures. They grew up amidst the warm fields, through which wended sluggish rivers. They were warm; they were expressive. Their dusky faces and bright-colored garments were suggestive of passionate embraces. On more than one occasion Lemnas had caught the Autharian girls looking at him. Boldly they gazed upon this blond youth, who blushed and turned away. Lemnas found the cold peak of his brain melting beneath the hot glances of these flatland maidens.

The getaway, therefore, had been something of a relief.

They trudged through the marshes and Lemnas forgot his feelings. Now they were returning, however.

One of the herders was a girl of voluptuous physique and the same frank expressiveness. Lemnas looked across the backs of the cattle and there she was, Telyal. The rustlers had again provided a welcome diversion. When it was over, Lemnas had felt concern that Telya might be injured. He was relieved to discover that she was fine. She caught him looking around. When he saw her he stopped searching, and she had laughed. Her white flashing teeth and red lips beneath her cloth scarf plunged Lemnas into the same trouble as before.

Now at the watering hole, Lemnas marshaled his feelings. He sat on a grassy mound back from the water. Telya and a young boy splashed the cool surface. When she climbed out, Lemnas discovered that the garment she was wearing was see-through. Lemnas felt something happening to his throat, and when he cleared it the sound was hoarse and odd.

The little boy played with Telya. They splashed each other and laughed. Other cowherds came to the watering hole. The older men were distracted with their reckoning. Telya climbed out of the water, pulling her wet garments away from her skin.

He heard Artemis calling him for dinner. He shouted vaguely back to her and gave a wave. Artemis went back to the campfire. He lay on his back. The blue sky stretched out about him. He dozed. He felt something tickling his face. He waved it away. He felt it again and opened his eyes. There was Telya and a couple of scamps dangling a strand of hay over his face. They giggled and dangled it again. He waved his hand away.

"Where do you come from?" asked one of the boys.

"What? Away from here," said Lemnas.

"He comes from heaven," said Telya seriously. "His blond hair is like Perchta's." She ran her fingers through his hair.

The little scamps took issue with this. "No, he doesn't!" they shouted. "He comes from the west."

"Who says?" she asked, looking not at the boy but at Lemnas directly.

"Master Viho," said one boy.

"No, he didn't," she said.

"He did. He did!"

"Anyway he's here now." She continued to look at him.

"And where are you from?" asked Lemnas, looking up at them.

"Not far from here. Ten miles." There was a shout and she turned swiftly around. Without pausing she jumped up and ran away. The scamps scrutinized him for a moment longer, then turned also and ran away.

When Lemnas returned to the campsite he found the Thuringians engaged in urgent discussion. They sat beneath a cluster of three tall hornbeam trees. They had a fire going and above it hung a pot for fruit broth. This was a beverage prized by mountain folk. They drank it after meals. Artemis nodded at Lemnas's plate, which she had covered with another plate to keep away the bugs. The boy, still distracted, went over to a log and sat down. He picked at his food and put it down again. He listened to what was being said.

"I don't understand you!" cried Ajax in mystification.

"You were never as devoted to Perchta as some of us. Not to say that you're impious, but just simply, it's not your character. Otzi, Tribal Chief of the Thuringians, is more of a seat-of-his-pants type guy," He screwed up his eyes in perplexity.

"Well, it's like you said," replied Otzi, "our good fortune depends on the Moon Goddess. Even I understand that much. For this reason I believe that we should pay a visit to the Terrwyn Henge."

"Ordinarily, of course, I would agree," replied Ajax, still frowning with suspicion at Otzi.

"Well, and from what you've told us, we've been lucky. Very lucky."

"You're right," said Ajax. "Had we not had the fog the night we escaped from Trilock's, it is doubtful we would have gotten away."

"Perchta," submitted Nestor.

"A few minutes ago you were accosted by Zeras's men. Your spell of concealment is all that saved you."

"I said a prayer to our silver-footed Goddess of concealment," murmured Ajax.

"Who cast a veil over the searchers' eyes and minds," Otzi continued, nodding.

"Thank Perchta for that," agreed Ajax.

"If we are to get farther, we must continue in this vein. We must make an offering at Terrwyn Henge."

"The soldiers are fast on our tracks. At the Kula, we offered our ceremonial gift. Perchta will have taken note. The Autharians did not give theirs in return, as is the custom. But this of course was because we decided to leave, rather hastily."

"There were reasons," objected Otzi.

"Granted, but Perchta will not blame the Autharians."

"Maybe she will, maybe she won't," returned Otzi stoutly.

"I guess, my question is: why now?" Ajax looked at him dubiously. "We are in a desperate hurry. If we don't get back to the village, our friends will face Trilock's men unaided. They will have no advance warning beyond what our lookout can give them. The mere thought turns my blood cold. Yet now you wish to dally by the shrine!"

"Perchta, who looks down on us, sees us as mere ants. She laughs at our stratagems, our crawling progress. We can't hope to win out if she does not favor it," replied Otzi blandly. Otzi, in spite of these terrible dangers, seemed to be in good humor. Ajax could not understand it.

"Don't you see it, lad," put in Nestor keenly. "Our Chief has something up his sleeve."

"Either that, or he has some piece of bad news." Ajax rubbed his chin considering. "And he can't bear to break it to us. He softens us up with a visit to Terrwyn Henge, which he knows I'll appreciate."

"Or both," added Nestor sardonically.

Otzi continued to smile, saying nothing.

"And of course he won't tell us," replied Ajax, still looking at his chief.

"Why spoil a good thing?" replied Otzi, grinning.

"Oh, you make me mad!" shouted Ajax, and jumped up. He shook his head and muttered. The big man walked off.

Artemis took the kettle off the fire. "And you can't tell us, I suppose?"

"Nope," replied Otzi. "Not yet."

85

Young Master Ossian

South of the Heckla River was a land ruled by a wise and benevolent tribal chief. This was Lord Crassus, whose country ranged from the hills to the west to the shores of the sea. For generations Crassus's family had controlled the area, here and there gaining or losing a piece, but always keeping roughly the same quantity of land. Under this ruler and his forebears the realm had grown rich and orderly. They maintained themselves through farming, through ranching, and through the production of handicrafts and other goods. The Carnellians, as they called themselves, did not look much beyond their borders, although they remained vigilant in the case of trouble. They maintained a standing defensive force which guarded the Carnellian bank of the Heckla and the hills in the south of the realm.

Crassus had a son, Ossian, who was the object of much devotion. The lord of the land valued the boy and was sure that he would grow to become a worthy heir. He was smart, he was high-spirited. He was, in addition to this, however, very restless. Ossian had from a tender age given himself over to mischievous pranks. He had put sneezing powder in the stew served at the castle, with hilarious results. At an official banquet he had crawled under the table, tying Lord Eklo's shoes together. When that august lord had risen, somewhat the worse for wine, he had taken a dive onto his nose. The table had tried their best not to laugh hysterically. As he gained in years, Ossian's mischief acquired scale. He succeeded in forging his father's signature on some official documents. These he and his friend presented to a sea captain. The captain was perplexed but an order was an order: Ossian and Vitello departed for the Western Ocean. Vitello and he had had a bet concerning the edge of the world. Once they got there, Vitello had pledged to throw a stone or some heavy object over. If they heard a splash, they would know that the world was indeed borne on an infinite ocean by great sea-going turtles. They never got to the edge, unfortunately. The Carnellian navy overtook the merchant boat and brought Ossian and Vitello home.

Crassus was determined to keep the boy under wraps. In a couple of short months, Ossian would be going off to Egypt to be educated. Once there, as Crassus hoped, the educational environment would have a calming effect on the lad. In the meantime, it was vital that Ossian not make another break for it. Crassus needed to keep him out of trouble until then. For the past ten days he had been confined to the castle as punishment for various misdemeanors. Everyone was going crazy. Crassus had to figure something out.

The Pursuit Continues

Zeras and his men crossed over into the neighboring realm of Brescia. There were few guards defending the border, yet Brescia was prosperous and valued her independence. The realm's leader did not think much of Trilock but did not interfere in or oppose the Magnificent One's schemes. Brescia was prosperous and hard-working. Around it were tribal lands, which contended with one another. Brescia kept to itself and tried to stay out of trouble.

Now, however, trouble had found Brescia. Zeras and his riders approached the walled village of Brescia Town. They were joined by another squad of ten, which had been patrolling the lands to the west. To these now also were added a hundred footmen, armed roustabouts impelled by Trilock's promise of gold. These foot soldiers stood in a line facing the town. The town's gates were closed and armed citizens stood on the walkway looking down over the wall.

The mayor of the town had put on his armored leather vest. "What is it you want?" he demanded.

"We want the criminal called Otzi and his villainous

associates," shouted back Zeras in a peremptory tone.

"Not here," returned the mayor.

"We want them," repeated Zeras.

"They are not here. And, may we say, we protest your coming into our land unbidden!"

"You will like what I do even less if we have to ask you again," shouted Zeras.

"We don't have this man you speak of," began the mayor. The man's fear was beginning to be evident. His defiant tones had about them something strained.

"Otzi."

"Yes, we don't have him! We don't listen to your threats."

"Threats," replied Zeras coldly. "Listen to you. They hear your cries of mercy and your vain pleas. Their only answer is the sword."

Zeras hesitated no longer. Before the mayor could reply, he nodded to his men. His second gave a shout. The footmen walked forward. In front of them were shields. The Brescians launched a volley of arrows. For the most part the shields blocked them. Arrows glanced off or became stuck in the shields.

Behind the men were the horses. Again the arrows rained down. When they drew close enough, the horsemen threw up grapnels. Several of these caught on the top of the wooden gate. The Brescians fired down another volley. One of the horses was hit and stumbled. Several footmen fell. Brescian soldiers tried frantically to pull off the grapnels. They managed to pull off one. The grapnel fell to the ground. But the grapnels were attached in the back by ropes. The horses turned and leapt forward going in the opposite direction. When they reached the end of the rope, they paused briefly. The rope pulled them back for the briefest of instants. The grapnels tore the door off its hinges before becoming detached.

The Brescians came charging out to meet the Autharian footmen. A battle began.

"Kill all those who resist," Zeras instructed his men. "Round up the rest. We sell them into slavery." He turned contemptuously from the carnage going on behind him. He had known that Brescia did not have Otzi and his associates. Zeras simply had needed to make an example of a tribe who resisted. The rest, as he knew from experience, would obey out of fear. Here was the beginning of a change in the way things ran in the area. Autharia would begin to dominate the region, as Trilock long had planned. Let them deal with these pesky mountain folk first and foremost!

The fighting continued behind him. The result was a foregone conclusion. It was simply a matter of tactics and the number of one's men. He heard the cries of agony and fear rising from the fray. Zeras consulted the map of surrounding lands and considered their next move. He reached his hand to his mouth and found a smile there.

"And if I let you do this, will you have the decency to calm down?" Crassus asked his son Ossian, who stood before him in the Tribal Chamber. Certain of Crassus's men stood at attention, while the ladies sat in chairs toward the back.

"But of course, father," replied Ossian suavely. "It's absolutely not a problem." Crassus frowned at the little reprobate, not believing a thing that Ossian said to him. The only ally Crassus now had was time. They had to keep the boy busy for another two weeks and then—Egypt.

Crassus smiled. Ossian smiled. They appeared each to understand what the other was thinking.

Crassus nodded to the stout guard, who came forward. "They will be going to the circus, as I understand?" he looked to his son for confirmation.

His son nodded.

"See that he doesn't join the circus."

"No, sir," replied the man.

"It will be difficult, I know," confided Crassus to the bodyguard. "Don't let him out of your sight."

"I understand, sir," replied the man seriously.

"You have two weeks!" Crassus glowered at Ossian. "And then—"

"—Egypt." Ossian finished his thought with a mild, somewhat injured smile.

"All right. You may go. Here, take this money." Crassus nodded to the Treasurer, who came forward with a pouch. Ossian snatched up the pouch of coins and ran out of the hall.

"Well, after him!" demanded the tribal lord, shaking his head.

"Yes, sir!" replied the man and bounded after his charge.

A Kindly Act

The next day the cattle drive continued on its way. Lemnas looked across for Telya. Several boys her own age had joined the girl. They appeared to be brothers or cousins, and Telya joked around with them much as she had the young scamps. She did not turn in Lemnas's direction. Gooch and his friends continued on their way, and Otzi and the Thuringians herded the cattle. From the rustlers Otzi and Ajax had acquired horses. These they now rode. Artemis and Lemnas walked with switches in hand while Nestor rode one of the more peaceful steers. The day was very hot and the party broke but up ahead was a forest.

The drive passed without resistance through the forest. The same path had been trodden bare, while on either side tall trees grew up in thick groves. Sometime in the early afternoon Gooch signaled for a break. The mountain folk, who were not used to the heat, sought refuge in the woods. A little path led into the darkness. There, after a hundred yards, they came across a creek.

People were there already, some women washing garments. Two men, idlers or else unoccupied farm hands, leaned against one of the thick tree trunks. Otzi watched as a little boy made his way down the path, which ran along the stream. He was an odd-looking little fellow, with a large head and limbs that were strongly developed for his age. He must have been eight or nine. The basket he was carrying contained persimmons gathered from somewhere in the woods. He did not look at any of them as he passed. He passed close to where the idlers were standing. One of the idlers suddenly stepped forward and kicked the basket out of the boy's hands. The basket fell on one side and the persimmons spilled out. The women looked up, shaking their heads. The idlers laughed uproariously.

"So sorry, Garo," said one of the men.

The little boy, called Garo, said nothing and began to collect the persimmons. As he did so, the man moved forward again. He stepped on the boy's hand as he reached for a persimmon. The boy cried out.

"Thug!" cried out Otzi, who pushed the man backward. The man tripped on a branch and fell. The other idler snarled ominously.

When he saw the idlers kick the basket out of Garo's hands, Otzi had climbed to his feet. He knew at once that he could not let this pass. The Thuringian approached from off to one side, where he would not be observed. He knew well enough that the idlers were not through with the boy.

The second idler stepped forward and took a swing at Otzi. Otzi ducked and punched the man in the chest. Then he kicked the man in the stomach, causing his opponent to double over. The first idler, meanwhile, had climbed to his feet. In his hand was a short, solid log. He swung at Otzi also. Otzi leapt back. The mountain folk made no movement. They knew that the chief could handle this.

Otzi was backed up against the tree. The man swung again but the log connected with the stump. Now Otzi stepped forward, pushing the man's overextended arm in the same direction it was going. Off-balance, the man tried to shift his legs. But Otzi put forward his left leg and leveraged the man off of it. The man fell into the river. The second man groaned on the ground. Otzi made a threatening gesture with his fist but the man waved his hand in submission. The shaken idlers took themselves away from the scene.

Otzi began to help the boy to collect the persimmons. The washerwomen clapped and applauded the actions of Otzi. At the same time, they appeared to Otzi to seem a little apprehensive.

"You're all right, are you?" said Otzi, patting the boy on the head.

"Yes, sir. Thank you!" said the boy. He was a good-looking little fellow, if still unlike the people Otzi had seen in the lowlands. When they had gathered up the fruit, the boy looked up. They saw an older man with a limp coming along the creek.

"Thank you, sir," said the man, hobbling up. He bore some resemblance to the boy, Garo, thought Otzi. He had the same large head and heavy limbs. This man was on the old side but, more than anything, his foot hobbled him. Along his ankle was a scar he'd evidently sustained long ago.

Ajax came up now. He and Otzi shook the man's hand. "I am Volney," said he. "You have saved the boy from two well-known bullies."

"You should stay away from them in the future," advised Otzi. "They're a nasty pair all right," said he affably.

"We will indeed. Please, sir, as a token of our thanks,

may I give you this?" To their astonishment Volney had produced from his pocket a little talisman on a chain.

It was a singular-looking charm, with markings on it the mountaineers did not recognize.

"No, no thank you. It was nothing.," replied Otzi, waving his hand in refusal.

"It was far from nothing.," said the man with peculiar emphasis. "Please. Please, we insist."

"Oh, well, if you insist," Ajax put in, with a smile.

"That's all right, old son. We'll take it," said Otzi's second good-humoredly. The man grinned and nodded. It had been important to him to give them the charm.

"We will go now," said the man with an apprehensive glance farther down the path. "Blessings be upon you!" He took the basket from Garo and took the boy's hand. The boy looked back as he was led away.

"Hmm, strange," said Ajax, examining the charm. "The old prong really wanted us to take it."

"We're in the lowlands," replied Otzi, clapping his friend on the shoulder.

"Anything may happen." Ajax nodded and they went back to the others.

The cattle drive continued into the afternoon. They came out of the band of forest and were once more in the plains. Artemis was scrutinizing the other ranch hands. In addition to her superlative skills as an archer, Artemis was very perceptive. She had noticed with amusement Lemnas's little dalliance with the girl, Telya. She had further observed Nestor's clumsy efforts at talking with the boy about it. Although still young, Artemis understood people intuitively. She did not like what she was seeing now.

There was an ominous change in mood amongst the

other ranch hands. Gooch, because he no longer looked in the Thuringians' direction, inadvertently confirmed this. The day was bright and tall, billowy clouds hung low across the sky. Bel, the Sun God, drove his mighty carriage across the heavens. The animals trotted east along the broad bare swath of the drive.

The town of Brescia lay smoldering in ruins. Although this was satisfying, it was not an end in itself for Zeras. He watched as the women and children were led off in chains. He was thinking of the effort to locate Otzi. They had been conducting sweeps of the countryside, going back and forth. So far nothing had turned up. Otzi was resourceful indeed!

One of his scouts came galloping back to him. He saluted Zeras and brought his horse to a halt close to him.

"Our search in the south yielded nothing. Chased a couple of leads, but nothing resulted."

"Like what?" Zeras looked up from his map.

"Oh, had a couple people on a cattle drive."

"What did they look like? How many?"

"I don't know, fifteen, twenty all told."

"Appearance."

"Varying, some young, some old. There was a big guy but he did not match."

"What did he look like? Exactly!" An idea was germinating in Zeras's mind.

"Well, he was big, burly, muscled. Dark hair, cut so long."

"Bearded?"

"No."

"Did you notice his face? Was it bruised at all?"

"Yes, come to think of it, here." The scout put his hand to his right temple. "But it's not the guy you mean."

"Ha!" Zeras came beside and grabbed the man's hair affectionately. "You fool, you idiot. You dupe!"

"I am happy to be mistaken," said the other man with an irritated grin.

"Then you are a happy man indeed!" shouted Zeras. He whistled for the others. They turned at once and came to him. "We move now!"

"At least tell me what it was."

"The Moon Goddess has been playing tricks on you, Loogan."

"What—" Loogan began, but already the horsemen turned toward the south.

In Thuringia

The mountain valley glittered in the midafternoon sunshine. Above it to the east stood peaks that rose to heights thousands of feet above the lowlands. The higher reaches were bare of vegetation and snowbound. The lower slopes were covered with dark forests of spruce and fir. Still lower were bright green pasturelands, and amidst these pastures was Thurin Village. Here was the homeland of the mountaineers led by Otzi the Iceman. For a place so high up, the village was relatively large. The town consisted of seventy or eighty houses. There was a main street; there were adjoining streets and walkways. A bridge led over the stream which came down from the mountains. On the west side of the valley was a sheer mountain face, rising perhaps a thousand feet. Great boulders gathered at the foot of this sheer cliff.

Life in the village in the summer was pleasant. The Thurin Pass saw many travelers: northerners, southerners, strange folk from lands to the east or west. So long as they paid their fee, they were welcome to come along through. Scouts from the village guarded the pass and prevented unwanted or nonpaying wanderers from making the journey. It was thus that the village had prospered down the generations.

Otzi, the tribal leader, was gone to the Ceremonial Kula but life proceeded in an orderly fashion. Fruit was gathered from the fields, and shepherds plied their trade. Otzi's wife, Ana, was busy as well. She might be the village chief's wife, but this did not absolve her from the obligation to work. Ana kept their modest home scrupulously clean. She helped to shear the sheep of the upland valley. She milked the goats and made cheese. She gathered water from the stream and toiled industriously in the vegetable garden. She had begun to introduce their young son, Gula, to these tasks. He liked the sheep and wanted to help shear them. Ana missed Otzi awfully. To keep her from feeling gloomy, the other women came by for tea and to pass the time. They enjoyed long evenings before the fire, knitting garments to help ward off the cool mountain air. The spacious cottage now accommodated seven or eight of the local women and girls. They watched as the menfolk returned with a load of wood for the fire. Ana brought forth from the hearth a raspberry pie, and Ana's guests all laughed and clapped. Otzi, if he hurried, might return to eat one of the remaining pieces, thought she.

Taking Leave

"I think you should leave," Telya stood close beside Artemis in a turn in the cattle path. Bushes sprung up by the side of the path concealed them from the others. Otzi, Nestor, and Ajax came up. After some hesitation Lemnas joined them.

The girl was serious. She spoke hastily; she looked apprehensively around her. The other ranchers might double back at any moment.

"The men which you beat were some of our kinsmen. They are shiftless, not good workers. They don't tolerate being beaten, however."

Otzi understood it all at once. They were speaking of the men who had been bullying the boy. "The ranchers are planning some revenge."

The girl stood before them, unsmiling. There was none of the coquettishness of the previous day. Lemnas could not understand this person, at once so childish and so adult. Far more adult than he, he would have to admit. The girl had approached Artemis, not Lemnas. Lemnas frowned and considered what it was she was saying.

"We will wait for the end of the day."

"No, go now!" she insisted. "It doesn't matter. Master Gooch will not stop them. They know that you are sought." She cast a quick glance apprehensively up at Otzi. Up to now she had been speaking only to Artemis.

"Sought by whom?" Otzi asked. He wanted her to say it.

"Sought by the Lord Trilock's men," she replied without hesitation.

Otzi nodded. "Thank you, we will go at once."

"Thank you," said Artemis. She grabbed Telya's hand in an uncharacteristic display of affection. Telya squeezed it back, turned, and was gone.

"Back this way, I suppose," suggested Ajax, and they followed him through the bushes. The bushes formed a long row that served the purpose of breaking up the fields. Probably also they protected the crops from the wind. They walked along this.

"Terrwyn Henge it is," said Otzi, with a grin.

"How far are we?" asked Ajax, appearing to consider the prospect for the first time.

"Not more than five or six miles, according to the ranchers."

"I still don't get you," complained Ajax, and they walked down the lane.

Terrwyn Henge

"You must be out of your mind!" cried Ajax as the mountaineers approached the famous henge. They had been walking across well-tended fields. In the distance they could see the winding path of the Heckla River. The band of water shimmered a bright gold in the afternoon sun. As they grew closer to the famous religious site, the land became untended. Now there grew up a combination of grasses and light-colored trees. Birch and alder fluttered in the breeze.

But Nestor was not thinking of the sacred place they were about to visit. He was thinking of Otzi's words.

"Orcus." Otzi nodded proudly.

"You want to go into Orcus?" Ajax repeated, himself not believing it. Lemnas felt a surge of excitement, while Artemis fingered the end of one of her arrows.

"Indeed. Well, 'want' is perhaps a little strong."

"You think it will save time?"

"I know it will."

"How can you know!" demanded Nestor. Nestor seemed to consider the idea a bad joke.

"They do say that Orcus is a shortcut to the mountains,"

explained Ajax. "They also say that it is deadly. It has an evil reputation."

"If we don't do this," replied Otzi, "our friends are dead. Our family members, dead."

"They can fend for themselves," countered Ajax.

"Unlikely," put in Artemis.

"We'll talk about it later," Ajax said, and fell silent. He could see that Otzi had thought of the visit as a means of getting on his good side. Ajax valued nothing on this Earth higher than the blessing of Perchta. The Terrwyn Henge was an ideal place to make offerings to the Moon Goddess.

The trees and tall grasses fell away. Ajax stopped to stare at the awe-inspiring sight. The grass here was cut very short. The sun gleamed brightly over the smooth expanse. In the middle were upright stones, or menhirs, of gigantic proportions. Beyond it lay the Heckla. A steep bluff fell away from the Terrwyn Green. The stones formed a circle. Each stone rose to a height of thirty feet. Hands of great strength in centuries past had pulled these stones to this place. They had buried them deep and secure in the ground. The menhirs loomed above them as they approached.

The others were silent too.

"Perchta, Goddess of the Moon," offered Ajax solemnly. "Aid us in our perilous journey. Protect our village from the attentions of our enemies."

He walked slowly toward the center of the Henge. Otzi followed at a respectful distance. Otzi was essentially offering Ajax and the others a trade. In exchange for this visit to the Henge, he was requesting that they follow him into Orcus. The feared realm was accessed by a yawning gap in the Earth some ways north of there. It was a subterranean realm with wondrous creatures and strange folk. Not many who went down into it came out again. It was also, though, as Ajax had surmised, a shortcut to the mountains. They would not get back to their village in time unless they tried something extreme, unless they went into Orcus.

Ajax needed a few things to perform the appropriate ritual to Perchta. "Gather up some gairea and mistletoe." He was instructing the others. He stood in the middle of the circle of menhirs. There was a stone table here, giant in proportions. Ajax had climbed up onto the table and was searching through his pack.

The others had gone off into the grasses and trees to look for Ajax's ingredients.

Ajax couldn't do anything without them. He looked contemplatively up at the menhirs and up at the blue sky. He cast a sidelong glance at Otzi from where he lay on the stone table. "You're getting into a gray area, Tribal Chief," he said with a quizzical smile. "Trading favors for Perchta. Not a good idea."

"Unfortunately, I doubt that Perchta will have much pull in Orcus. This is a place where the Moon does not shine."

"Do not joke! Perchta is more than just the Moon. Besides, all you had to do was ask."

"Really?" Otzi chuckled.

"No," scoffed Ajax. "Orcus? Nestor was right. You're crazy." He looked up at the peaceful sky. He ruminated. "Lots of adventures. Do you ever get tired of it?"

"Ah, my friends," came a voice from behind them. "I hope you prayed to our gods too." They turned to see Zeras and his men. They had crept up silently, hidden from sight by the looming menhir. They had stepped out from behind the stone, their weapons drawn. There were twenty of them at least. Nestor, Lemnas, and Artemis were nowhere in sight.

Otzi drew his blade.

"Weapons, is it, friend Otzi? Your impiety is troubling," quipped Zeras. The foremost military man of the Autharians smiled. Otzi recognized the expression from the interview with Trilock. It was a cruel smile, devoid of sympathy or what usually passed for humor.

"Well, here you are," said Otzi, whose mind was racing with calculations. Ajax sat up, his feat dangling off the front of the stone table.

"Yes, we thought we'd find you here. That was a nice trick of concealment." he addressed Ajax. "Loogan was none the wiser. Fortunately I have some knowledge of these sleights of hand."

"So was that it?" Otzi demanded in a loud voice. He found Zeras's confiding, victorious tone difficult to bear. "The salt trade. That small purpose is what motivates your master?"

"Yes. But you know it's not a little thing. It is a big thing. My 'master,' as you call him, probably will become the force in all the flatlands. There will be none to oppose him."

"You don't think the others fell for your little set-up job?" scoffed Otzi. He noticed that the soldiers were fanning out. They wanted to encircle them. *The river!* thought Otzi. This was their one and only chance. The far edge of the green ended abruptly in a steep drop-off. Forty or fifty feet below the Heckla rolled on its way.

"It doesn't much matter what people may suspect," Zeras shrugged. "They can suspect, and they can act. Personally I was sorry to see the Chinese Ambassador go. An amusing fellow. But this was the price."

"You will kill us?"

"Oh certainly. To intimidate the tribes," nodded Zeras. "We will put your head on a stick. Ajax, how about you?"

"Mine on a stick too, please," joked the big man.

"Done," replied Zeras, and stepped forward.

Otzi rolled to the right. Ajax flipped backward across the stone table. These were small movements, achieving seemingly little. The first arrows missed because of them, however. Otzi rolled underneath the table. He was between the two stone uprights. Another arrow tore into the dirt next to him. He was out the other side and running. Ajax leapt off. An arrow passed into his shoulder. He fell down with a grunt, got up, and kept running.

The Autharians were not mounted. They had walked forward to escape notice. They ran forward as well. It was a sprint to the bluff. Arrows flashed around them. Otzi and Ajax ran in zigzag motions. They were close, they were oh so close!

Zeras let fly a throwing knife. He roared in frustration. The knife found the back of Otzi. It ripped into his backpack. The Birchwood uprights of the supports blocked it from going further.

The water splashed around them. It was cool and powerful. The current was stronger than it appeared on the surface. Otzi and Ajax were plunged in its green-brown depths. They knew that they must stay under as long as possible. When they were underwater, they could not be seen.

Their lungs were bursting. They had to come up. They surfaced with a gasp. "There!" they heard above and behind them. Three arrows whizzed around them. They went down again.. The next time they were much farther away. Another arrow sought them out. It splashed down twenty feet from them. They went down again. The next time Ajax and Otzi surfaced, Zeras and his men were no longer at the top of the bluff.

The water surged along. They needed to stay in the middle of the current to outpace the Autharian soldiers. They began to relax. The water was cool and around them it was quiet. However dangerous things appeared, Otzi had noticed, silence had a soothing effect. They were in the middle of a river on a sunny day. Ajax leaned back. Otzi noticed that a trickle of blood issued from his friend's shoulder. He became concerned. Otzi saw a branch coming downstream behind them. He paddled against the current until the branch caught up to them and took it toward Ajax, who was treading water. They both held on to the branch. They wondered where their friends were. Thank Perchta they had not been with them!

An arrow dropped down, becoming stuck in the far end of the branch. In panic they looked to the shore. Were Autharian men still pursuing them? Ajax laughed. He saw, attached to the shaft, a sprig of mistletoe. It was a message from Artemis.

They began wading toward the shore. A sandy beach fringed the Heckla here. They dragged themselves out. Lemnas and Artemis jogged up to meet them. A minute or two later, Nestor joined them.

Lord Trilock stood at the door of his suite and appeared lost in thought. There was a flutter of wings and a pigeon landed on the top of the table in the courtyard. He went outside and gathered up the bird. He removed from its talon a rolled message. He put before the bird some feed and a little bowl of water.

Trilock considered the message. He walked absently into the room. Through a double door could be seen the supine form of Sincha. She wore a leather choker around her neck. A blanket was thrown carelessly over the lower half of her body, exposing her chest and arms.

"What's the word?"

"They've let them slip. Now the Thuringians are over in Carnellia."

Sincha perked up at this news.

Trilock considered the message. He crumpled up the rolled piece of birch bark and looked across at her. "Zeras has gone over into Carnellia to get them."

"Isn't that against the rules?"

"I imagine," he said with a calm smile. "Not getting this Otzi is also against the rules. Failing to win the situation is against the rules too."

"But chaining your girl to the bedpost—that's not forbidden?" Sincha of Leponto reached up and pulled against her neck choker. The chain clinked.

"Not only not forbidden," replied Trilock, as he approached the bedroom, "but actively encouraged."

The Inn

The Thuringians had crossed the broad waters of the Heckla. They had grabbed hold of logs and waded across. The day was getting on and darkness soon would be falling. Ajax grimaced as they climbed out of the water. Artemis had removed the arrow, including the head. The waters of the river had cleaned the wound. They had put some wool from their pack into the wound to try to prevent it from bleeding.

"There's a town not far from here," said Artemis, taking Otzi aside.

"How do you know?"

"The ranch hands were telling us."

"Artemis is right. Carnell Town. It's big," seconded Nestor authoritatively.

"We should clean the wound. We should get into town."

"I can hear you!" called out Ajax in annoyance from a tree stump some distance away.

"It's for your own good!" called back Otzi.

"I'm fine," he said, and tried to shake off the wound.

"Let's go before it gets too dark," nodded Otzi.

Several miles downstream on the other side of the river, Zeras contemplated their options. They would have to go over, that much was clear. Otzi was nearby and nothing was more important. *War with Carnellia was preferable to failing to get him*, thought Zeras drily. Nevertheless, they would want to keep a low profile if possible. From the local people they had pulled a few garments which looked less "official." They paid a boatman to get them across. The horses they would stable on this side. They would make them far too conspicuous.

***

The mountaineers had walked the several miles south to bring them to the outskirts of Carnell Town. Their clothes had long since dried and the evening was well on. Carnell Town was a sprawling village, larger than any Thuringians had seen to that point. The city walls were strong but old and not kept up. They had been worried that they would find the gates closed to them for the night. But the gates did not close at night and no one guarded them. Wagons full of goods came and went and people walked in and out. No one paid much attention to the travelers from the north.

The streets were well lit and on every corner was a tavern. They wanted to be inconspicuous so they moved off the main thoroughfare. On a side street they came to a cheerful, well-lit place. The downstairs was a tavern and the upstairs seemed to have rooms for travelers. The tavern keeper was accommodating and brought them upstairs.

Ajax they left alone in a tub to soak. He had a bottle of something fiery from the bar downstairs. The big man refilled his glass. Artemis and Nestor grinned to hear a saucy tune issuing from the bathing room. Her patient seemed to be progressing well.

The others went downstairs into the common room. They felt relief that they were now in a different land. Carnellia was an upright and substantial realm. They doubted whether Zeras and his men would try anything.

Still, Otzi considered, this did not solve the considerable problem of getting north again. They would have to go through Orcus.

"What is Orcus?" Lemnas asked as he ate the chicken and potato in front of him.

Nestor sipped at his glass of ale.

"You know as much as I do," replied Otzi. "Legend paints it as a desperate, dark place. I expect it's pretty well exactly that."

"It is in fact dark, no, because it's underground?" posed Lemnas.

"It's light," replied Nestor with assurance. "There is light."

"How can that be?" asked Lemnas, mystified.

"There are many strange things in the world, boy."

"That's so," replied Lemnas thoughtfully. Just take the foregoing days, he considered. What now would become of Telya, he wondered. She would be fine; probably she would marry another of those ranch hands. For the reason that she had approached Artemis with her important information, Lemnas felt that he understood the situation better. She was part of a tribe, and that meant not going outside one's tribe.

Lemnas had not considered much whether he behaved that way, until now. As he thought of the matter, he reflected that he did not. He would not mind a girl from another tribe. Probably the specific location of Thuringia helped him here. Day in and day out, Lemnas gazed upon the mountain heights surrounding them. The mountains, so distant and so cold, concerned themselves little with human affairs. When one considered this fact, the life of a man was not worth so very much. One ought not to be consumed by little tribal squabbles. One ought to like whomever one liked, friendly tribe or otherwise.

"Have another, boy," Nestor nudged him.

"What?"

"Another pie," said the kindly, avuncular figure.

"I'm fine," replied Lemnas with a shrug.

"We need you at your best, lad," insisted Nestor. "Full of action. Orcus lies ahead."

Lemnas shook his head, appearing to consider this destination unlikely.

Otzi was thinking of the foregoing days. He wondered about Sincha. Had she been part of the setup? Probably, in part, but Otzi understood divided loyalties. People who were entirely loyal were suspect. Or else, they were lacking in spirit. Otzi was a man of the mountains, it was true, but he did just like a bit of an adventure in the broad, wide world. There was action down here, and Otzi liked action. The soft feel of Sincha's waist came back to him. She might not have been with him, just as he was not with her. He would try to justify that small fragment of interest which she had shown in him.

He smiled to think of it. Nestor stretched and seemed ready to call it a night. Lemnas, while wishing the old avuncular presence a good night, caught sight of a pretty barmaid. This girl was a blond, and she was surveying Lemnas with more than the usual interest.

Zeras Incognito

"Here is some medicine," said Artemis, sweeping into the room. She flung the pouch carelessly in the direction of the hungover Ajax.

"Where have you been?" asked Otzi, perking up. He had been drinking broth and was sharpening the blade of his sword.

"Oh, about," she said airily, flopping down into a chair. They noticed a difference in the girl. She seemed pleased with herself, and beyond that, she looked different.

"You're wearing makeup!" Lemnas observed, having detected a reddening pigment on her lips.

"Yes," said Artemis. She grinned. "There's a circus in town. I imagine this would interest you." She looked at him scornfully. "Sweets and such."

"I am not a child!" retorted Lemnas. Ever since the rather indifferent result with Telya, Artemis had reverted to speaking to him as if he were twelve.

"What, an actual circus?" Otzi perked up.

"Yes. I imagine. They come from the Far East."

"From China?"

"Not that far. Near Egypt. They have lions and elephants."

"Sounds interesting," replied Otzi.

"It would be, if we did not need to get back to our village without delay," put in Nestor churlishly. Nestor did not like to be excluded from any form of amusement, and he seemed to think that a circus would exclude him.

"You're right," replied Otzi, thinking better of the idea. The gravity of their situation came back to them. Outside on the street were the cheery shouts of tradespeople doing business. Somehow it was exciting. Ajax bestirred himself from the bed. They would have to continue their journey that very day. Otzi's plan was to travel by night. They would attract less attention that way. It was going to be tricky all the same. The Autharians had sent word out far and wide. If ever they managed to get north into the foothills, then they could decide about Orcus or the overland route. Either way, Otzi did not like to think about it.

They sat downstairs in the dining room. Otzi looked grave. "Eat up," he said. "Get seconds."

"Pushy, pushy," replied Artemis, who was still in a festive mood.

Otzi cleared his throat. "Unfortunately I have some bad news." They stopped smiling. "This meal represents the last of our funds."

"What?" demanded Lemnas. "How?"

"Our money pouch seems to have fallen out when we were crossing the river." "Seconds it is." Ajax held up his plate for the waitress to refill.

Young Ossian sat on the couch in the official residence of Carnell Town. Vitello and Hoska were there with him. Ossian's friends had adopted that blasé manner which is peculiar to hangers-on in all eras. They looked at the ceiling. They made themselves little sandwiches of cheese and carrot. Ossian was conscious of the impending deadline. Only a few more days before his dreams of adventure were to vanish forever. He knew how it was. The schools in Egypt were full of young braves like himself, desperately intent upon making a break for it. Annoyingly, the school was in the middle of a desert, five days' walk with no water in any direction. Ossian and his fellow students would never make it out of there. They would have to get down to studying.

Carnell Town had been his last hope. Vitello had suggested the pretext of the circus. It was unfair to ask his friend for another idea. Ossian had to make something happen on his own. The bodyguards were watching them like hawks. The chief guard, Darkus, was not such a bad fellow. He could be funny, and he would supply them with alcohol if begged. On the other hand, Crassus had demanded absolute security on the threat of loss of livelihood. Ossian would have bribed Darkus, but he did not have access to that sort of wealth.

"So. We go to the circus?" asked Hoska, whose young leg was bumping up and down in restlessness.

"I suppose." Ossian went to look for his shoes.

"I can make some money at the circus," suggested Lemnas when they were gathering their things.

Otzi looked over at him curiously. "What makes you think that?" he asked.

115

"I asked the barmaid downstairs. They have a knife throw."

"Oh, hitting up the barmaid!" Artemis teased him with a grin.

"Why not?" asked Lemnas. "A man has his appetites." The others laughed at this.

"Wonderful," Otzi shook his head. "It's too risky. Zeras's men could be around."

"You think?" Ajax perked up.

"I do," replied Otzi gravely.

Lemnas pretended to agree. He slumped down on the couch again. Otzi and Ajax went downstairs to get some supplies with their few remaining coppers.

"Where you going?" demanded Nestor, when Lemnas got up.

"Nowhere," he replied carelessly.

"Don't be going to the circus!"

Lemnas shook his head dismissively, as if to say that he, too, had heard Otzi's instructions. It was therefore unnecessary for Artemis to repeat them. Lemnas sauntered down to the main dining room. He went to the garden out back. When he was sure no one was watching him, he quickly hopped the wall and was out in the streets of Carnell Town.

***

Zeras and his troops sat in a tavern in the town center. Zeras was not drinking but felt a need to keep ordering. They must not attract suspicion as they sat there in the morning sun. The ale they drank was dark and rich. His men drank sparingly, for they were under the watchful eye of their leader. Next to them was a very drunk man.

He had not been drunk when the morning started. The table next to him kept handing him beers. He could not understand it. It was like some life other than his which he was leading for that day. He was careful not to object, however. The men in the next table took away the man's empties and put them in front of themselves.

"I see one, sir," called out one of the soldiers.

Zeras did not move his head. "No pointing. Where?"

"Over your left shoulder. It's the young lad."

Zeras pretended to drop a utensil. While stooping to pick it up, he looked back. It was the mountain boy, all right.

"You three, after him. Keep your distance! This operation depends on guile. We can't have the entire Carnellian Defense Force coming down on us."

"Yes, sir."

The men rose. In order to make themselves appear as casual as possible, they pinched the bottom of the waitress. She snarled at them good-humoredly.

The Circus Act

The circus was a wandering band of traveling Sumerians. They owned a ship by means of which they sailed the Mediterranean. The ship was something out of fables: it housed man and beast alike. It also housed the famous beast-man, whom the people paid their good money to see. The ship was theirs thanks to a bet. Their wily, enterprising leader had won it in a game of cards. Nine months in the year they traveled from land to land. In the remaining months they visited their families and scouted for talent.

Towns that accepted them did so on certain conditions. The circus needed to set up well outside the town limits. They also had to hand over some of their proceeds to the appointed officials. They had been in Carnell Town for the past month straight. It was a nice spot, for people all over the region did business there. Farmers, traders, day workers spilled out their extra coppers on sweets and the dancing elephant act. Lemnas grinned with pleasure as he approached the gate. The barmaid had lent him three coppers on the understanding that he would return her investment if he was successful. Lemnas had assured her that the knife throwing was a can't-miss proposition.

Everywhere he looked there were booths with some new object of fascination. But he tried to block these all out. He needed to focus. Lemnas had absolute confidence in this one skill—knife-throwing. As with anyone who was in possession of a supreme skill, Lemnas felt that life held no obstacles in store. One had simply to win that one thing, knives hitting a target, and all else melted away. Lemnas would win a few coppers to get his tribe to Orcus. Beyond that, it was all adventure. He could not believe in the peril of Orcus, because he was confident of victory at the circus booth.

There it was ahead of him. Prudently Lemnas had remembered not to bring along his own knives. The punter might recognize him for a ringer and debar him from participating. Less prudently, indeed, Lemnas did not bother to look around him. Had he done so, he would have seen three rather serious men following him at a distance of twenty paces.

Vitello and Ossian walked down the main thoroughfare of the circus. Vitello looked about him, somewhat desperately, for some little straw of diversion to point out to his prominent friend. Hoska was somewhere around. He had promised to rejoin them in a few minutes. Ossian was feeling crushingly bored. So this was how it all ended up, he was thinking. One seeks the ends of the Earth and one finds a lane full of stuffed dolls and snake girls. Behind him walked, as ever, the bodyguard. Darkus was growing more confident with each passing day. The dream of freedom was closing up for Ossian with every minute that passed.

They heard shouts from the end of the lane. A crowd had gathered. Still uninterested, they sauntered in that direction. Another shout went up from the crowd. They saw the punter first, looking flushed and nervous. On the one hand, the man would be concerned that he was losing money. On the other, he was excited to have his contest validated in the eyes of the public. Vitello disappeared into the crowd. Ossian looked about for him. The chubby farmers' daughters were stuffing their faces, always more of the same. Off to one side he spied three men who did not match the scene. They were gaunt, powerful, and unsmiling. They were grizzled and chipped with scars. Beneath their workaday garments Ossian saw weapons. What did this mean? His interest, at last, was piqued.

Vitello came rushing back to him. "You have to come watch!" he said, with an excited smile. Still looking at the tough-looking men, Ossian allowed himself to be dragged toward the front. The farmers instinctively made way for them. Darkus followed behind, simply pushing the common people aside.

They saw a booth, and next to the railing up on a footstool was the punter. The man wore a bright blue costume. His coat stood in marked contrast to his cheeks, which were flushed with excitement and damp with sweat. Before them was a boy, probably their own age. He wore a faded rustic outfit which did not suit him. The boy held in his hands several knives. He balanced one tip down on his finger, which was in of itself fairly remarkable. A target shot out behind the counter. It was being controlled from below by a man who pulled levers. Too quick even for sight, the boy grasped the handle of the knife and threw it at the target. The powerful impact of the blade's impact proclaimed the boy a winner.

The audience cheered loudly. They began to chant for an encore. The boy smiled but not, as it seemed to Ossian, to the crowd. He was smiling to himself. He smiled in response to some ongoing train of thought in his head. Another target appeared. Straightaway it was skewered.

The boy already had cleaned out the punter. The audience wanted more. "Farther back!" shouted someone from the crowd. The punter looked at the entrant questioningly. The punter worked for the boy now. The boy took several steps back. It was a difficult distance. A target appeared, and the result was the same. Ossian was captivated.

For years he had been seeking some partner in his travels. The young scion's journeys had been more or less imaginary, but always had it seemed indispensable that he should have a partner. Here was a young lad like himself, pulled it seemed from one of the stories his parents had told him when he was little, so lithe, so young, and so capable.

"Farther!" demanded the audience.

"Last one!" replied the punter, who was mindful of not overtaxing the young champion. The boy stepped farther back. Now the throw was incredibly long. One could barely see the target. The distance was not less than fifty feet. Silence preceded the test. They waited. The lackey who pulled the lever seemed to want to build the tension. Down below, he hesitated to pull the lever. There it was! The audience waited for the painted squirrel to stop quivering. A knife lay embedded in its belly. The crowd cheered uproariously! They clapped between his narrow shoulders. The punter pushed them away and took the lad by the arm. He led him to the money box. He wanted one and all to see that he dealt fair and square with the customer.

Lemnas, as he was being led toward the booth, caught sight of Zeras's men. He could not think. His mind went blank. He felt bitter regret that he had engaged in so foolish a competition. As money was being thrust in his hand, he felt an arm lock into his. A well-dressed young enthusiast was trying to hustle him away from the crowd. Lemnas had to get away from Zeras's henchmen. He allowed himself to be pulled.

A Hasty Departure

Lemnas sat sedately in the house used by Ossian, son of Carnellia's ruler, Crassus. He was curious about the guards who seemed to watch the young scion's every step. Vitello played a game involving round wooden pebbles with Hoska. Lemnas watched it absently, not understanding the rules. He did not much care about it and he did not understand why he was here. He was relieved only to be out of the way of the henchmen who had been following him. But how was he to get back to the inn without attracting attention?

Ossian, meanwhile, was trying to appear calm. Often he had practiced this, particularly in the preceding months, because he was so much under scrutiny. He found it amusing to reflect that the first, say, twelve years of his life had been devoted to drawing attention to himself. The more recent five had been devoted to deflecting attention. What would be his next phase, he wondered? Whatever it was, he wanted to put it off for a while longer. Here was his opportunity, although he did not quite know how to make use of it.

"Then what happened? They spotted you at the

Henge?" Ossian prompted Lemnas. Lemnas had been regaling Ossian with tales of his exploits. He did so partly out of nervous exhaustion. It would have been too tiring to make up new stories. He wanted to ask his contemporary for help, but he felt uncertain of the response. Ossian seemed to be guided by motives not easy to read.

Ossian had an instinct about the situation. He must get Lemnas out of the hearing of his friends. He did not trust his friends when there seemed to be some prospect of his actually achieving his aims. "Here, come and have a look at this," he said, drawing Lemnas along with him. Darkus seemed tempted to follow them, but he refrained. He remained standing in the doorway of the living room. Ossian took his new acquaintance out onto the balcony.

They looked out over Carnell Town. It was a handsome town, with spires and well-tended gardens. Ossian and Lemnas stood beside each other. While Ossian pretended to point out sights, he murmured under his breath to Lemnas.

"Don't tense up," he said in his undertone. "They'll notice. You are still being pursued. Am I right? Don't nod or shake your head."

Lemnas said in the same hushed tone "yes" while he pretended to lift his head to sun himself.

"We go. Right now," he said. "Don't look down. Trust me that the drop-off is only a few feet. We run back to the circus and hide in a place I know."

"Before we do that," said Lemnas, getting into the swing of it. He laughed and shook his head in seeming admiration of a remark by Ossian. "Before we do that, tell me why you want to escape."

"My father, Tribal Chief of Carnellia, is sending me away. I want to go to Orcus and be in battles and other such things."

"Right," replied Lemnas to a reasonable explanation. "And when do we do this?" "We do this in ten seconds' time."

"Good," Ten, nine, eight, seven...Vitello and Hoska sat intent upon their game. Darkus looked at the ceiling. How he could use a drink, he thought. But when this was over —

The boys jumped over the balcony. "Bel!" Darkus rushed forward in a panic. He looked down, expecting to find them limping off. The drop-off, to his surprise, was only a few feet. The hill stretched steeply down. The young men were running out the gate to the garden. Darkus shouted to the others. They ran off in pursuit.

The henchmen of Zeras had reported the events at the circus to Zeras. Now Zeras and several of his men sat not far from the official residence of Carnellia. Zeras was tempted simply to raid the house. The sight of tough-looking henchmen who appeared to be patrolling the compound dissuaded him, however.

He was trying to come up with a backup plan. Perhaps, because of the danger, Otzi was making some arrangement with the Carnellians? Maybe the Carnellians had agreed to let Lemnas stay for a period while Otzi attempted to return to the mountains. If that were the case, Otzi might very well be on his way again. Zeras was considering doubling back to watch the river and return to patrolling the north bank of the Heckla.

They saw the mountain kid and the young Carnellian lordling run out the back of the house.

"Quick! After them!" he shouted. His men leapt up

and ran off in pursuit.

The circus was winding down. The concession stands had a ragged look. The customers, worn out, footsore, and blasé, walked slowly down the lanes as they moved toward departure. "Hey, watch it!" cried out a lady as the two young men tore back into the camp. Following close behind were several tough-looking men. The men cared not at all for the customers. They pushed them over, upset carts, and barreled their way through.

Up ahead was a temporary stage. It was made of wood and built for performances of magic and dancing. Ossian knew the ins and outs of the place. In the first days he had attempted to befriend the manager in an attempt to secure passage to the Rock of Gibraltar. The manager and no one else was in sight. Ossian and Lemnas jumped up and leapt behind the curtain.

The bodyguard of Ossian leapt up a few moments later. It was so dark back there! There were a hundred props; they could not make sense of it. Mirrors and unfolding boxes and cages with wild animals in them shocked them. A hyena laughed mockingly as they passed. Then they found—Zeras and his men. The men grappled briefly with one another, for it seemed to them that the other group was trying to abduct their young man.

Zeras needed Lemnas, and Darkus needed Ossian. They drew their weapons. A crowd, meanwhile, was gathering outside the curtain. Word of the chase had reached the ears of the manager.

"I am a manager!" called up a man from below the stage. "Come out of there! You are not permitted!"

Exasperated, Darkus pulled aside the curtain. "I work for Crassus," he said. He pointed to a Carnellian badge. The manager put up his hands and left them.

Darkus looked keenly at the other, Zeras. "So?"

"You have a missing boy, and so do we."

"What's your plan?" asked Darkus keenly.

"To find them, and save our jobs," replied Zeras.

The Thuringians had gathered together their gear and were now ready to go. The plan was rudimentary: they would walk farther east along the river. Several miles downstream, when they were out of sight, they would cross the river and move north as darkness came on.

Their packs were securely fastened. Ajax, Artemis, and Otzi were assembled in their room. Nestor came in from the bathing room. He too was ready for the journey ahead.

"Where is Lemnas?" asked Ajax.

They heard a commotion outside and a sudden rush of feet. Lemnas and a young man they had never seen appeared in the doorway. They were in a high state of excitement.

"Here!" cried Lemnas and plunged down into a seat. "Oh, and this is Ossian," he declared with a prideful smile. "He'd like to come with us."

The Thuringians and young Ossian paddled across the river to the north side. No alarm had gone off in the town. Ossian explained that the henchmen would not want to risk revealing that they had lost their charge. They would want to recapture him, Ossian, before his absence was noticed.

"You think they have joined up with the Autharians?"

"I do," affirmed Lemnas.

Ossian explained that they had escaped by means of a trap door in the floor of the stage. Ossian had agreed to help them get out of Carnellia, on condition that they helped him to escape. Otzi was by no means inclined to grant this request. Lemnas pleaded with him at length. Lemnas would not have managed to escape the henchmen had it not been for Ossian. But he should not have been out anyway, objected Otzi!

Lemnas wordlessly plunked down a pile of coins won at the circus. "We did not need this!" Otzi shrugged.

"It's easier though," urged Ossian suavely. "I assure you that Vitello and I would never have gotten as close as we did to the Edge of the World without being amply provided with coins."

Otzi paused. He was going to object further but thought better of it. In fact they did need money, and Lemnas's exploits were amazing by the sound of it. Also, Otzi did not like to come off as a crotchety old man. Lemnas and Ossian chuckled as they recounted to Artemis and Nestor their recent daring escape. Otzi later would assure Ajax that he planned to send the young scion back to his father at the first opportunity.

Trilock and the Tribal Chiefs

rilock the Magnificent sat in the Council with other chieftains from the area. The chieftains were discussing the usual business of the late summer, such as crops and the threat of invasion. Roaming predatory bands sometimes descended upon the area, and in the event the chieftains came together to repel them.

The session had proceeded slowly. Trilock had the impression that some of the members were looking at him curiously. They sat in a small amphitheater, no more than twenty yards in diameter. The steps were constructed of wrought stone. During the break Trilock's neighbor had turned to him. "So sorry to hear what happened at your Kula."

"Thank you. It came as a great shock," replied Trilock sorrowfully. "One lets these people into one's home, and they take liberties."

"But you are confident of apprehending the criminals?" pursued his neighbor.

"Very much so."

"A Thuringian, is he? Name of Otzi?"

Trilock nodded. "Yes."

"I would leave no stone unturned, I tell you." The man shook his head with vexation.

"I assure you, we haven't," replied Trilock. "His hours on this Earth number but a few."

The others nodded, pleased with this display of confidence. Above all they required order to be maintained. The death of the Ambassador, while tragic, could be smoothed over if the criminals were apprehended. But they did need to be apprehended. Trilock's position on the Council depended on it.

The journey through the Alps Mountains was long and arduous. The road was difficult and steep at first, then leveled out, and then became steep again. The military men under Lord Trilock were approaching the completion of the middle stage. They had proceeded with untiring energy at the start. They grew weary as the middle stage continued, yet still they did not stop. Two horse-drawn carts carried their supplies. The men walked freely, each with a weapon at his side. This man carried a sword, another a hammer, yet another an axe. Each of these tools of war had spilt the blood of enemies. The mountain area fell prey to a sudden rainstorm. The water came down in sheets and the road grew muddy. Suddenly it was barely possible to continue. They had brought a cart, drawn by horses, for supplies. They found it very difficult to drag the cart through. The men shouted to each other above the din of the torrential rain. They crouched beneath their coats and paused, debating how to continue.

It was then that the first arrow hit. A man went down, the shaft protruding from his chest. The others drew their weapons and scattered. The others hid behind rocks, behind trunks. The arrows came thick and fast. They came from all directions. Trilock's men were skilled campaigners, however. They did not panic. They waited for a pause in the onslaught. Then their own archers stepped forward and aimed. Two, then three bodies fell beneath the counterattack. The attackers did not show themselves. They fled. The ambush was over. The leader shouted to the men to pull the cart out of the mud. Strong backs turned to this task.

The leader and his second approached the body. They pulled aside the headgear. It was a man, scruffy and mud-flecked. He bore no insignia indicating to whom he would have shown allegiance.

"Thuringian?" asked the second.

"Doubtful," commented the leader. "Thurin villagers are more organized, from what I understand, more prosperous. This man is a scavenger, a fugitive."

"Why would they attack so big a convoy?"

"They saw the rain coming, they had been following us. If we'd fallen back they'd have had our supply wagon."

"They bit off more than they could chew?" asked the second.

"They did." He left the body where it lay. "We move on at once!" He shouted to the men. They were making progress. Thuringia lay ahead.

Ladies of Leisure

Ochsana, the female chief of the Vahetians, considered her options. Vahetia was a realm far to the east of Autharia. The Vahetians did not owe the Autharian leader, Trilock, anything, and neither did they fear him. The Vahetians were a warlike band composed entirely of women. They rode splendid steeds brought from the east, which gave them a great advantage in battle. They were powerfully built, tall, and athletic. They engaged in all manner of athletic competitions. They could do as they liked when demands were made upon them by neighboring tribes.

The day before a small group of riders had asked permission to come over into their territory. They approached on horseback, the dust rising over the dry, grassy plain. A man, Zeras, stepped forward to talk. He was straightforward enough. Perhaps sensing that threats were not going to work in this case, Zeras had offered money, a lot of it. They were looking, he said, for a band of fugitives. Ochsana had already heard something of this. She did not let on, however, and let Zeras say his piece. She promised to consider his request. Zeras and his men had galloped back in the direction they came.

The travelers wandered over a scrubby, unfarmed land north of the Heckla. The sun beat down on the dry yellows and greens of the untended plain. The group traveled at night to avoid being seen, and they stayed off the main roads. They were getting closer to Thuringia. As they did so, their thoughts turned to their friends and family at home. They hated to consider that they might arrive a few hours late. They were doing their best, but Trilock's forces would be far ahead of them. The option discussed by the group was looking more and more likely.

Ossian was having a fine time of it. He liked these people and their urgent purpose, it was like his own, and yet was utterly unlike it. Ossian's quest was in response to his own need for personal growth. These people were concerned about their loved ones. They knit their brows and walked stoically forward.

For the most part the Thuringians did not talk much. Old Nestor had spun for him a few vivid tales from his youth. Utterly implausible as they were, Ossian expected the others to chuckle. At most they ventured a half smile before becoming serious again. With Lemnas he grew bashful. His contemporary had rendered him an invaluable service in helping him to get away. But Lemnas was no mere novice in the arts of fighting. His knife-throwing had proclaimed him amongst the highest lights, though he was still young. Ossian was conscious of a gap in achievement between himself and the young mountaineer. When he approached her, Artemis looked at him with austere condescension. It was going to be tough to break the ice there.

Mainly he chatted with Ajax. Partly it was that Ajax and he were in clearly distinct weight classes. Ajax was a light heavyweight, a brawler. He had powerful limbs and that easy way of moving common to muscular, well-conditioned people. Ossian was a featherweight. Actually the boy liked to think of himself as more of a strategist. In the future he would lead such men as Ajax into battle. In the meantime, he had to gather knowledge. He played up to Ajax at every opportunity.

"And so," he said, as they walked the trail at dawn. They had been on the road for several hours. Ossian was not in the least bit tired. He continued. "When you were fighting this brute, you relied on what? You say he was strong?"

"Very strong."

"You're strong too," pointed out Ossian.

"Not like that," replied Ajax, with a chuckle.

"Then your speed? Paint a picture for me!"

"You rely on your plan," submitted Ajax. "I'd take advantage of my speed, yes. But this only takes one so far."

"Go on."

"He's going to catch you, guaranteed. He knows it and I know it. The plan therefore is simply to withstand that one punch."

"Interesting."

"You see, if I go down, he wins. If I don't go down, I win."

"I don't understand."

"His one conviction, the one thing he knows, is that he can put anyone down. He's been doing it all his life. Now, if I take that shot, what else has he got?"

"He's still very big, a bruiser."

"He's still big but he's not unique. In uniqueness lies a man's hope."

"I feel that, instinctively, to be true," assayed Ossian boldly. "I mean, I don't know. I suppose that's why I'm on this adventure with you fellows. Why, what's this?"

"Hello there," replied another voice.

"Hello, ladies," said Ossian with a gallant smile.

The Thuringians had been walking alongside a grove of tall trees. The land around here was mixed grassland and stands of forest. They came beyond the stand and they met a retinue of beautiful women.

***

The Vahetian woman spoke in a low and measured voice. The group was now seated in a canvas tent. It was held up by poles which had been lashed together. Inside was it quite high and spacious. It was comfortable: couches were provided for seating, carpets, and burning censers for light. The tent could probably be broken down in an hour, which was of benefit to the nomadic Vahetians. The furnishings provided lasting comfort, and the interior was pleasantly shaded from the fierce sun.

Otzi sat across from a woman, tall and clean-limbed. She sat in a folding chair and looked over the group. "I am Ochsana," said she.

"And I am Otzi. We are traveling to the mountains." "Through our land, though you might not have known it."

"You are right, ma'am, we did not know it. Our journey was not planned, say that much. We apologize for intruding. Now, however, we must get north to our homeland."

Ochsana paused in scrutiny of these travelers. She was tanned and athletic from habitual exertion. Probably she rode with the other women in all their expeditions. Across her temples she wore an elaborate diadem befitting her rank. She smiled, not with kindness, but with appraisal.

"You are being pursued. Yet still you hope to get away."

"We do," replied Otzi with a frank smile.

"Yet escape is, it is apparent, very unlikely."

"We are not without resources or stratagems," returned Otzi.

"We know your pursuer. We know his strengths."

"What is this man's name?" asked Otzi.

"His name is Zeras," Ochsana replied, looking directly in his eyes. Otzi felt that she was trying to will him into inaction. In some part of his mind he was reminded of Ajax's trick with the soldiers. He paused, resisting the Vahetian's will.

"Is this some kind of concealment trick?" asked Otzi. "Does Perchta help you now?"

"No," replied Ochsana. "It is a Vahetian delaying trick. Zeras is not even an hour away. You are on foot. You will be caught."

"What!" cried Otzi, leaping up. "Away!"

The ladies moved to restrain them. A big girl grabbed Artemis by the arm. Artemis, strong as she was, struggled to free herself. The girl looked directly into Artemis's eyes. She appeared also to be willing the mountain girl into inaction. Artemis felt the pull of kinship with this warrior female.

"Do not resist," said the strapping girl. Artemis pulled, but felt in two minds. These women were so proudly independent! Yet no, she had allegiance to her village. Of

136

course she did. She pulled again and the other did not let go.

Ossian ran headlong into Artemis's opponent from behind. "Oof," he cried. He had not done so intentionally; he'd just been trying to get away. The girl's grip relaxed and Artemis pulled herself free. Ajax ducked away from two girls and Nestor ducked out the back, where no one expected them to exit. They did not follow him. When he looked around, he saw his escaping friends.

"Nestor!" shouted Otzi.

"Wait for me!" yelped Nestor.

They ran through the forest, where arrows could not find them. The Vahetians did not make much of a show in following them. Their purpose had merely been to delay.

Ossian sat on the same carpet where Otzi had sat an hour before. He was drinking a fragrant decoction prepared by the ladies.

"I think this could work out well," he assured the Chief of the Vahetians. "You are women, and I am a man. You don't, I am guessing, need a lot of men. You just need a couple. Or even one."

"You would become our honorary man?" replied Ochsana, looking at him closely.

"I would. I mean, this is the kind of thing for which I am admirably suited," he said, with a wink at the Chief. Ochsanna laughed.

The tent flap opened and Darkus and the other bodyguards came in.

"Ah, Master Ossian," replied Darkus with an affectionate smile.

137

"What?" demanded Ossian of Ochsanna in a wounded tone.

"Sorry, darling," said she, as her second accepted a sack full of coins. "I'm all about the money."

"I felt we had something," replied Ossian, still lingering a moment longer.

"Check back when you're twenty-one," said she.

"Yes!" Ossian replied in triumph. He pointed at her, his thumb jutting horizontally out, as if by this gesture indicating that person with whom he had a special bond.

For now, though, it was off to Egypt with young master Ossian.

Into Orcus

Otzi and the others ran through the forest. They knew that Zeras was not far behind. They had simply now to get to Orcus. It was odd to think of Orcus as preferable to their current situation. From long experience Otzi knew that, sometimes, moving into greater danger was the plan. Better the greater danger than the present one!

They followed a path heading north into the hills. They came into a broad grassy reach. It was worrying to be so visible but they had thrown caution aside. They needed only to get to the entrance to Orcus. They were confident no one would follow them in there.

"You know where it is?" asked Nestor.

"I do," replied Otzi. Nestor did not ask for explanations.

Zeras examined the broken stem of grass that lay in the path. The dirt was dry and there were few prints.

"You know where they're going?" asked one of Zeras's men, Loogan.

"I do." Zeras rubbed the stem between his long fingers.

"Then where?"

"Orcus."

"And where are we going?" asked Loogan nervously.

Zeras turned. His face broke into a brilliant smile. "Orcus."

The mountaineers climbed into the hills. The humps of the hills were grassy, while the canyons were heavily wooded. They walked down into a canyon. It was cool down here and the ground was moist and leafy. They felt a cool breeze from ahead of them. The canyon turned a corner and there it was, a wide black crack in the earth. They could not see into it. Otzi struck his flint and lit one of the torches he had purchased a few days back in Carnell Town. The oiled rags burst into flame and they walked forward.

The ground was loose, bare dirt for the first hundred yards or so. Then the surface turned to bare rock. A tunnel led forward, then dropped down steeply. The walls were dry and they did not find the footing tricky. After walking for about a mile, they met a stream, which crossed the path. They walked carefully through, holding on to each other. The stream bed was slippery but they managed to get across.

On and on they went into the darkness. They were afraid, certainly, yet they knew that this represented the only chance of getting back to their village. A distant chance it was, yet they had to try it. Desperation prompted them to overcome their fears.

They walked forward and down, then met a wall. It seemed at first that they had come to a dead end. Ajax called out to them and they saw a narrow hole in one corner. They hesitated before continuing down this hole. On the other hand, what did they have to lose? They went down. The way was steep and tricky. They had to look for finger holds as they went down. Next they came across something that surprised them. A kind of moss of lichen began to grow on the surface. It was moist and spongy. They were not so far from the surface that they could not think how it survived.

Otzi slipped. He was off, sliding down the chute! The others tried to catch him but to no avail. He gained speed and slid out of view.

"We must follow him," declared Ajax.

"No, Ajax!" said Artemis. But Ajax had already let go and commenced to slide.

Otzi slid swiftly down. The wet moss was very slick and there was no means of reducing his speed. He swept across a corner in a long turn. How long he slid he could not have said. He hit a flat section but was going so fast that he did not stop. He seemed even to be going uphill, but still he kept going. Suddenly he was out again, tumbling end over end on something soft. It was sand, white sand, and he was out in the open. He climbed wearily and disbelievingly to his feet. Just as he stepped forward Ajax came shooting through the hole. He narrowly missed Otzi and skidded to a stop, spitting sand out of his mouth.

"Well, well. Tribal Fearless Leader." Ajax smiled wryly at Otzi.

Otzi grinned. "You can't say this trip has been boring."

Ajax shook his head and climbed slowly to his feet.

"The others followed you?"

"I hope so," Ajax replied. He stepped out of the way. A minute later the others came down as well.

What a sight greeted their eyes! They were in a vast open space. It was not a cavern, unless the whole center of the earth could be described as a cavern. They had come into a new realm. They were on the fringe of a broad sea. There was a fresh breeze about them, and as they looked up a bright white light hung in the air at a great distance. The upper reaches were wreathed in mist; the mists constantly swirled and the light was of varying shades of gray. Behind them was the high wall of a cliff. This cliff rose until it was lost in a mist above them. The water lapped rhythmically against the shore upon which they stood.

"Don't ask me where we are." Ajax shook his head.

"Orcus," suggested Otzi.

"Maybe," replied Ajax.

Then they saw something that alarmed them. Some creatures stood away from them at about half a mile's distance. They had seen them and were rushing toward them!

"Weapons!" cried Ajax.

The creatures were great fin-backed lizards, many times the size of men. They were covering the distance between them at great speed. In less than a minute they had grown close. They wanted to eat them. There were five of them, approaching them in a line. They looked at them cruelly, as they would at any prey. If, for a moment, Otzi had thought of running out into the water, he had to give up that notion. From the water came three more of these brutes, slowly rising up from the surface. The water streamed off them as they came onto the beach.

The first group stood in front of them, while the ocean-borne lizards approached from behind. Escape seemed impossible. Just then they felt some arrows fall down around them. It was Zeras and his men.

Otzi had to think quickly. "Concentrate on one, but stay alive. Let us injure one of them. The second one." Artemis fired a couple of arrows at the second one. The arrows sank into the scales of the creature. The lizard did not seem greatly troubled and moved forward again. The lizard snapped quickly at them. Otzi darted just out of the way. Then he ran forward, eluding the jaws of the second one. Flanked as it was by the others, the second one could not move out of the way. Otzi was on its underside and he stabbed upward. The lizard gave a grunt and leapt forward. The sword, still plunged in its belly, was wrenched out of Otzi's hand. He rolled to his feet and turned to face them. One of the lizards had grabbed Artemis by the sandal. It pulled her forward. Artemis grasped at the sand, but the sand did not give her back anything firm. Artemis's fingers left streaks in the sand as the lizard pulled her forward.

But then the lizards smelt blood. It was the flowing blood of their companion. Without another thought they turned upon the second lizard and plunged deeply into its flesh. The second lizard leapt away but not far enough. Agonized shrieks followed as the other seven lizards piled into it, ripping and biting.

"Quick! While they're distracted," called Otzi and they all commenced to run farther down the beach.

"Haste! Do it, move. We go now," shouted Zeras, whose men ran in a wide half-circle around the feeding lizards. They continued. Otzi and his crew were about a half-mile ahead. Otzi was approaching the cliff which lay behind the beach. He seemed to have some purpose in mind. "Quicker!" demanded Zeras.

Otzi had seen something in the distance. There were openings in the cliff face. They appeared to be caves at a height of forty or fifty feet. From the openings dangled creeper plants. They reached the cliff. He pulled on the vines; they were firm. They were pale green, in hue a little unlike the plants of the lands above. Without further ado Otzi began to climb the creeper. He pulled himself up without difficulty, while with his feet he sought footholds in the sheer cliff. In a moment he had reached the cliff mouth. The tunnel led back out of view. He called down to the others to follow. After Ajax came Lemnas. Nestor could not pull himself up by himself. They told him to hold tightly, securing one creeper in a loop around himself. The three pulled Nestor to the top. Artemis meanwhile had climbed another creeper. When they had all reached the top, they began to cut the vines.

Zeras and his men came up but they were too late. The vines lay in a heap at the bottom of the cliff.

"Sorry, old friend," Ajax jeered at him from above.

"You will be," declared Zeras.

"You better find another way out," Otzi cautioned him.

"Or else you'll be lizard feed," chimed in Artemis, and they all laughed. This was an accurate assessment. The lizards had already consumed most of their fellow. Bones of its ribcage and great finned back stuck out from the carcass. Soon the creatures would be in pursuit again. Zeras forbore from further comment and nodded to the others. The group all went rapidly down the beach.

Otzi watched them go. "Getting the better of him just never gets old."

"We need to make a move ourselves," Ajax reminded them. They looked back into the cave. They walked back into the darkness. They had only one torch left. Just as it was dwindling, the cave started to lighten. They came out the other side of the mountain. They blinked as they looked out upon the graying light of Orcus.

They were in a narrow canyon leading downhill. There was vegetation here, but of an unfamiliar kind. The plants had a tough, fibrous quality. There was no grass. There was, rather, an abundance of an ankle-high plant resembling oxalis covering the slopes. They looked up and saw additional strange creatures. Enormous featherless birds floated high in the air. Their heads were long both in front and behind, and they appeared to exceed in size even the largest eagle. The group looked apprehensively at these creatures, fearing attack from above. One of them did swoop low over the valley. They got a closer look. Its skin had a leathery toughness and its wingspan was ten feet or more. They ducked down protectively beside some rocks. The bird gave them a pass and swept by in search of other prey.

The Peaceful Valley

They entered a broad and fragrant valley. Large cactus-like plants grew in abundance on the upper slopes. In the bright light of the "day" they put forth yellow flowers. The plants were of a variety of colors: green, pale blue, and, here and there, red. Otzi and the crew took a moment to breathe in the mild air. In the distance was a grove of enormous trees. From these hung creepers similar to those which grew in the cliff faces.

As they looked up at the light, they tried to make sense of it. They were, by their reckoning, "upside-down." They were looking, not at the sky, obviously, but at the center of the Earth. Artemis recalled that at the end of the chute they had seemed to be going uphill. Their speed was so great that it carried them through. Gravity had flipped, though they could not understand it or even put it into words.

They reached in their bags and brought forth some food.

"Not sure if any of this is edible," speculated Nestor, looking around.

"The animals eat it."

"Up to now the animals seem to eat only each other." One of the enormous leatherwings circled high in the sky above.

"That's the center of the Earth, is it?" repeated Otzi.

"Don't ask me," shrugged Ajax.

"Yes, it's the center of the Earth," answered another voice, a deep voice, from behind them. A large man stood up and confronted them. He carried in his hands a heavy spear. He did not look friendly.

⚔

The natives to this land of Orcus had spied the foreigners the moment they had come out of the ravine. They maintained lookouts high up in the trees. Usually these were to watch for enemy Orcan clans, but they were adept at spotting surface dwellers as well.

A party was selected to intercept the strangers. They crept from bush to bush, then hugged the ground as they grew close. The strangers had not noticed their approach.

Now the natives surrounded the surface dwellers. Otzi and his friends leapt up and stood in a protective circle. They scrutinized these people who faced them. They looked different from themselves. They were strong-limbed with big heads and prominent foreheads. They had large, strongly defined noses and extremities. Although physically oafish in the consideration of the humans, there shone in the eyes of these natives the glint of intelligence. They were, in our modern vocabulary, Neanderthals. Thousands of years before they had vanished from the Earth's surface. Yet in Orcus these cousins of the modern human flourished.

"You will come with us," said they. They spoke with an

accent yet the mountaineers could understand them. When Otzi reached for his sword they raised their weapons. It was thirty to five. "No argument," warned the Orcan who had spoken first. Otzi took his hands away and held them up in submission.

The Neanderthals escorted the humans through the meadow and toward the far end of the valley. Up to now the visitors had been walking over rough ground, but now they met a discernible path. The path broadened as they reached the hills on the valley's far side. The path wound back and forth over this ridge into the next valley. This valley was equally broad and showed evidence of cultivation. Across the gentle slopes grew something resembling grapes. They saw Neanderthals working to prune these vines. These rustic people stopped to watch the humans pass. Neanderthal children ran in the lanes. They too halted and looked curiously at the newcomers. On the far side of the valley the saw evidence of a town. Closer to hand was a broad and massive building, constructed in the form of a pyramid. Otzi and the visitors took it all in with wonder.

Otzi had heard tales of Egypt and Babylon. He considered, based on these tales, that the Orcan Palace was more like the latter. The triangular outline of the structure was interrupted by a series of tiers. Each tier was smaller than the lower one, giving the building its pyramid-like shape. In the middle of the triangle, the "right angle," so to speak, was a long, steep flight of stairs, that the Orcan soldiers led the humans up.

Emperor Mog

The lands which Otzi and his friends had come upon were called by their natives Western Orcus. The subterranean lands were almost as large as the world above ground. There were seas, broad expanses of virgin territory, populous areas, relatively warm and cold spots. In the middle was the glowing globe which Otzi correctly interpreted as the Earth's center. The Orcans called this glowing source of light "The Orb." They gave thanks to it. There was a God of the Orb, to whom they prayed for all good things.

The soldiers escorted the visitors up the steps. When they reached the second level, they walked onto the platform. A large set of double doors opened. A stern and armored Orcan came out of them and approached the captives. Behind him were several guards in Orcan armor. Set into the foremost man's breastplate was a clear white stone of exceptional brilliance.

"Visitors, you are now in the power of the Western Empire of Orcus. I am Priceps of the Western Orcan Defense Force. Your presence here, for we recognize you as people of the Topside Realm, is strictly forbidden. You will now be incarcerated until your Hearing comes."

"Thank you, august and gracious Princeps," replied Otzi, in a clear, assertive voice. "We look forward to the hearing of which you speak. We ask only that it be soon, for we are in something of a hurry."

The Neanderthal guards had been drilled with the highest rigor. They stood, rock solid, on either side of the Princeps. Yet Ajax thought he could see the slightest pitying smile on the lips of one of them.

"Our trials are held when we think best. You will be informed of the Hearing when the time approaches."

He signaled to the guards and the captive humans were taken away.

Emperor Mog of the Western Orcan Empire was considering the difficult political situation in which he now found himself. The armies of Western Orcus had long been engaged in a war with the armies of Eastern Orcus. Of late the campaign had not been going well, owing to a number of factors. The weather had not favored them. Their Third Naval Fleet had been caught up in a freak hurricane and had been broken up. Those ships which had not sunk had been blown to distant seas. The expenditure of this war was great. The people had been getting restless. Mog had taken power a dozen years ago and people were beginning to talk of a succession.

The present Emperor had not come from one of Orcus's old families. He had risen from nothing, through sheer verve and cunning. Skillfully had he whipped up the passions of the common people. He had exploited unrest, and he had turned ancient families against each other. In order to keep the masses employed, Mog had undertaken huge construction projects. The Empire's debts were rising fast. To distract the humble mob from its troubles, Mog had launched a series of gladiatorial contests. Still things went against him. The aristocrats were fomenting rebellion. The clouds gathering over Mog's reign were beginning to look dark.

Yet to Mog, who was an excellent strategist, all was not lost. It was just a matter of figuring things out. He looked across over the valleys and mountains and could think of nothing. He rose from his chair in frustration.

Mog decided to pay a visit to his old friend Zak. Zak was the Imperial Armorer. The thick-necked old bull was getting up there in years. He had always been as an uncle to Mog, although a stern uncle. Zak was the finest swordsmith in the realm. One day Mog had gone in there. "Zak, you must give me that sword."

"No can do," replied Zak tersely.

"Who's it made for, then?"

"It is made for Roch, head of the Calavius tribe."

"Pah," Mog scoffed. "That's nothing. I will have that sword."

"No, you won't."

"I'll fight you for it," replied Mog haughtily.

"Will you now?" Zak was taken aback. He was an Orcan of the old school. He did not hold with whippersnappers coming into his workshop with their demands. Zak pulled out his own blade. "Let's see about that," he said.

Mog stepped away from the table. Whatever else might happen, they must not disturb Zak's workbench.

The room was broad and dark with low ceilings. Overhead thrusts were therefore out of the question. They fought. Mog stepped up and put his notched, unnamed blade close to Zak's neck.

"The blade is yours," replied Zak.

Zak looked up as Mog came in. The years had told upon him, yet still he was broad and powerful. "You looking for another sword?" he croaked as Mog came up.

It was their old joke. Mog chuckled. "No, just roaming the palace. Pondering."

Zak did not pretend to any knowledge of imperial affairs. That day he was working on a battle axe. He examined the side of the cutting blade for smoothness. "You need to get yourself a girl," the weapon maker grunted.

"I should. I got one, of course."

"You have three," replied Zak smoothly. "Which really means that you don't have any."

"Set me up." Mog grinned and shrugged. "Got any nieces I can have a look at?"

Mog wandered around the armory. He looked down the corridors. Here were weapons enough to staunch any invasion. How sad that he could not use them on the members of the opposing party! He heard a murmur of inquiry from the front. He looked out. There was a messenger. He nodded and the boy came up.

"Got some Topsiders, Sire. They're in custody. The Princeps wishes to know your orders."

"Be along in a minute."

"Heading out?" asked Zak, looking up briefly from the weapon's shimmering edge.

"Yeah, so find a girlie for me. What does it say that the Emperor can't find a date?"

"Sad times indeed," Zak commiserated.

Yet Mog, for the first time in days, was cheerful. These humans might come in useful. Mog had an idea.

The Western Orcan dignitaries gathered in the Grand Imperial Hall. This central meeting place accommodated a number of government functions: policy debates, important weddings, and trials. The humans had spent the night in the cells. They emerged with hands manacled. The gallery was full because human sightings were a source of great curiosity to the Orcans. Mog presided, while a council of elders offered advice. These worthies sat up front.

The humans stood before them. Next to them was their advocate, a scrawny fellow. He might be about average-sized for a human, but by Orcan standards he was but half-made. Guards on either side of them ensured that the humans were not going anywhere.

"Topsiders. I have been aboveground more than once in my life. From your fellow Toppers I know that Orcus is a name that prompts feelings of dread. If this is so, and we are merely curious: why have you come down here?"

"O Great Emperor!" replied Otzi, for he had been advised by his advocate to address Mog thus. "We know of Orcus's reputation as well. Please believe me when I say there was no other option. My people live in the Alps Mountains. Perhaps you have visited them?"

Mog offered no response to suggest that he had or hadn't. "Even now, as we speak, bad men are threatening our village with destruction. We knew of no other means of overtaking them. We wished to take a shortcut through Orcus."

Mog nodded. "We have no reason to disbelieve you. Your need, in all likelihood, was very great. You were also correct in thinking that you might get up the mountains faster."

The humans perked up at this. "Oh yes," continued Mog. "There are ways. Natural geysers serve as conduits to the surface. However, unfortunately, your journey was never likely to meet with success. Our laws are strict: we do not permit Topsiders to leave Orcus alive."

The Thuringians, who had been cheered the moment before, looked despondent now.

"What I will do for you is give you a choice in the manner of your execution. Do you choose the Orb, the blade, or a sharpened axe? There are many ways and this choice, in our land, is considered a luxury."

The humans were momentarily at a loss for a reply. Suddenly there was a commotion in the gallery. A guard was restraining a little boy who was desperately trying to come forward.

"What's this?" demanded Mog severely. The guard redoubled his efforts to get the boy to stay still.

The boy cried out: "Otzi! Show them the talisman."

Otzi turned around. He was mystified by the mention of his name.

"It is Garo!" shouted the little boy, who was pulled back.

Otzi remembered everything now. It was the boy from the glade near Terrwyn Henge! But what was he doing here? Nothing made sense. And what talisman?

"The charm!" cried Lemnas urgently. "He gave you something. The old man did!"

"Oh, oh!" cried out Otzi, remembering. He rifled through his pockets. This was difficult with his hand manacled but he had found it. He pulled it out.

Mog leaned forward angrily. He pointed to the little charm Otzi held in his hands. "Thief!" he cried. "Where did you get that?"

Otzi held it up for all to see. The markings, which had

appeared so strange, were commonplace in Orcus. It was a talisman bearing the Imperial Seal. Now an old man spoke up from the gallery. The travelers recognized Garo's minder with the lame foot.

"It was a gift!" he cried out now. "The boy is quite right."

"Bring them forward," ordered Mog. Garo and the old man were brought to the front of the hall.

"Sire, I gave the Toplander the charm. This man, whom I believe is called Otzi, saved the boy here from a beating by some bad humans. Did I do wrong?"

"No, Volney, you did nobly," replied Mog. "And certainly, this puts a different complexion on the matter. Our laws against intruders must be severe. On the other hand, a man who has shown himself to be a friend of Orcus is entitled to better treatment."

He conferred with the Elders for several minutes. Otzi looked down at Garo. Topside he had looked a little peculiar, but here he fit right in. Garo and Volney were evidently Orcans who traveled between the two realms.

The elders and Mog returned to their seats. The audience listened expectantly to what they would say.

"The humans are spared execution." There was a threatening murmur in the court. The mountaineers' spirits rose. Mog held up his hand for silence. "However, they are, in our opinion, unlikely to escape death. In order to obtain safe passage to their topside destination, they must encounter and defeat the Gygax!"

The audience gave a cry of surprise, then of disputation. Loud conversation broke out and the prisoners were led away.

Mog sat in his private chambers high up in the Imperial Palace. Broad windows looked out over the expanse. The sky outside was darkening but Mog did not feel sleepy. The assembly that day had gone well. Mog had intended to use the event to drum up support among the people. He did not feel strongly one way or another about the humans. It was true what he had said: he had been topside. As a young man he had gone there quite often. He knew those Alps of which the leading human spoke. There was a geyser that led to the very heights of them. He had found humans to be like Orcans, or a bit worse. They were vain, grasping, belligerent and petty, most of them. But, as with Orcus, there were some good ones. Perhaps these mountaineers fit into the latter category.

None of this would have prevented Mog from executing judgment upon them, however. This was the Orcan Law. Executions were always well attended. The excitement of the crowd tended to give the Emperor a little bump in popularity. He needed that for his struggle against the aristocrats.

But what had happened subsequently was even better for Mog. For an Orcan, and especially a sweet little Orcan like that Garo, to speak on behalf of the Topsiders was remarkable. The humans were cast into a sympathetic light. Let them now fight for their lives. The laws of Orcus were strict, and the humans could not have expected to be let off without a test. Mog considered it very unlikely that the humans would prevail. The Gygax was a fearsome beast. The humans would go down to a glorious death, and the people would be entertained. Mog would earn a reputation for clemency, and the aristocrats would be on the back foot again. He got up to fix himself a drink.

The Searing

The travelers returned to the cell in which they'd been placed the previous day. For some reason it reminded Otzi of their suite on Autharia Island. Well, not for no reason certainly: here they were formally prisoners, while on Autharian they had been informally so. In spite of the difficult situation they were in, Otzi found it possible to consider the Orcans dispassionately. There was much to admire in Orcus. Their level of handicraft rivaled that even of the Egyptians. Everything was well made, and the working people were industrious. The Orcans evidently had some knowledge of the "Topsiders," as they called them, and yet they did not desire contact with them. Were Topsiders really so objectionable, Otzi wondered? A lot of them were, certainly. Garo's intercession on their behalf had laid bare a sad truth: many Topsiders were unpleasant, unkind people. Garo had come to expect that sort of behavior. It remained a mystery why the boy and the old man had come up in the first place. Otzi was glad that they had. Had they not done so, he and the Thuringians now would be dead.

Ajax knew the foremost mountaineer well. He guessed

something of Otzi's feelings. "They seem to like persimmons, I expect," said he.

Otzi turned and grinned. "Can you actually read my thoughts?" he asked.

"More or less," replied Ajax. "You're thinking of Garo. Thank Perchta he was around, eh?"

"Hmm. I wonder if these people worship Perchta?"

"Hard to say." Ajax shook his head. "I can't imagine what their existence is like." They looked out the window. They had noticed that all the windows in Orcus had heavy shutters. They did not know the reason for this. Outside the light was dim. The time of day resembled night. This seemed to occur when the clouds that swirled constantly around the center of the earth became particularly thick. The light from The Orb was almost completely obscured. There seemed to be a pattern in the clouds' movements, perhaps not unlike Topside night and day. The "night" here was never pitch black, merely dusky. One could hardly see anything without torchlight. The Orcans had provided that for their cells.

The quarters were relatively comfortable. There were chairs and beds and blankets if they grew cold.

"What do you suppose this 'Gygax' is? Any clue?"

"None," replied Otzi. "Judging by the gallery's reaction it's pretty tough."

"Better to have a small chance than no chance," asserted Ajax, clenching his fish and unclenching it as he spoke.

***

"He did what?" Konno stopped, his bow poised for release. He allowed the tension of the bow to return to its lowest point. He palmed the arrow and turned to the man addressing him.

Konno, tall, thin, and imperious, stood in a dense forest on the edge of the Western Orcan Empire. He and his hunting party had been on the hunt for the past several days. Konno was deeply involved in politics and his advisers had suggested a vacation. Things were coming to a head, and it had to appear that Konno was not part of the plans now in full swing.

The outing had been productive. His hunting partners had bagged a total of fourteen Gyatian deer. A host of lackeys was on hand to dress and carry off the game. Now they sought something more elusive: the very swift Batati Bird. These creatures were not particularly beautiful or rare. They were, however, extremely fast. For an archer to bring one down was considered a lofty achievement. Konno had bagged three on this trip. He had been sighting out a fourth when the man had interrupted him.

Konno asked him to repeat what he had just said, very slowly.

"Senator," he replied, "it is quite true. The Emperor has set up a special edition of the games for these agile humans. The masses are excited and can hardly wait."

"This is simply unacceptable!" Konno stamped his feet. He thought for a moment. "Here, take this gold." He found coins in his pouch and pressed them into the man's hand. "I will be there tonight or in the morning. We will see what can be done."

The man nodded and departed.

Two other senators joined him. Hunting was forgotten. "Well, it's come to it," murmured one of the senators.

"We must object on grounds of procedure."

"It is in fact very rare, not to say unprecedented, to

allow a human to go free. Much less five of them."

"This Emperor thinks he can do anything. We must show him he's mistaken. And for a Topsider! My Orb! What next?"

The aristocratic senators jumped on their Fandos and set off at speed for the capital city.

Otzi and his friends were sitting in their room later that day when a servant came in. He was a plump, talkative Orcan with a clean-shaven face.

"Good morning, Topsiders!"

"Hello, Narto," the humans grunted. The man walked past them to the windows. He pulled the shutters shut and latched them.

"The warden feared that you would perhaps be unaware of our weather cycles here. Every three days the Orb is revealed in all her brilliance. At those times, we take measures to avoid her light."

"I see." Nestor nodded. So this was the explanation for the shutters. He remembered the tough bark and stems of the plants, which must have to be thick enough to withstand the light.

"What happens if you are caught out in it?" Ajax added.

"It's not pleasant." The servant shook his head.

"You seem, if I may say so, unusually friendly to us. We haven't had that."

"Oh." Narto laughed airily. "But you must understand that your situation has changed for the better. I am merely behaving accordingly. Combat with the Gygax is quite an honor."

160

"An honor?"

"It is." The man nodded with conviction.

Here was an opportunity, thought Otzi. "So, if you don't mind my asking, what is a Gygax?"

"Has no one told you? Well, I don't know if it's my place." He appeared to reconsider.

"It's all right," Otzi replied in an easy, joking tone. "We'll be killed no matter what you say. I'm certain of that."

Narto laughed too. "Well, since you put it that way. And, anyway, it's not much of secret. It's a ferocious furry creature that walks upright as we do. It is tremendously strong and tall, maybe twelve feet high. It's got blue fur."

"Blue fur, eh?" replied Otzi, in the same light tone and winked at Ajax. Ajax chuckled. "Sounds like a worthy opponent."

"I can take him," replied Ajax.

The servant laughed. "Well, look, I do wish you the best of luck. Anyone who is chosen for combat receives the highest commendation. You can have anything you wish for dinner, so just ask."

"Surprise us," chuckled Otzi.

"All right. I will." The servant left the room in the best of spirits.

"Wonderful." Otzi turned serious again. "What do we do?"

"I have a couple of ideas." They discussed strategy for defeating the monstrous Gygax.

Nestor came in an hour later. He had been having a nap. He noticed the light through the crack in the shutters, which seemed to have faded. "Oh look," he said. "I think the Searing is at an end." He undid the latch tentatively. The ground smoked visibly. The plants had turned their softer leaves away from the light. "Oh my," cried Nestor, looking out.

"Don't worry," assured him Otzi. "One way or another, we won't see another one."

Zeras and his troops had had a difficult time of it in the previous day. Yet now, it appeared, they had caught a break. After just missing Otzi and company on the cliff face, they had made a run for it down the beach. They did not like their chances against the finbacks.

As they ran, Zeras looked out upon the subterranean sea. He would have leisure to reflect upon this later. He wondered whether this land might be put to some use. There would be a time for these thoughts when the race was finally run. The ocean did not have any visible opposing shore. Who knew how far it extended? He heard an alarmed shout from one of the men. He looked back. The finbacks had picked up the trail.

Ahead there appeared to be something made by proficient hands. Was it—it was—a gate! It was a fence, high enough that it seemed to block creatures of the finbacks' size. They ran all out, their lungs bursting. The finbacks were almost upon them. They reached the gate. One man almost got caught but the finback came away only with his shirt. The lizards slammed clumsily into the fence. The gate was on the small side, but if they thought about it the lizards probably could squeeze through.

"Shut it!" yelled Zeras. The fence was jammed in the sand. They hastily began to dig. One lizard seemed to be forming an idea.

"Weapons out," called one of the leaders. They jabbed

at the lizards through the bars of the fence. One of them was bloodied. A moment before, a lizard seemed to be considering jamming itself through the door. The first smell of blood changed all that. Now all of his companions leapt on the bloodied lizard. The men managed to shut the door. It had a lizard-proof latch.

They watched with disgust as the lizards consumed their now-dead comrade. The beasts made loud smacking, snorting sounds.

"How moronic." Zeras shook his head and began to laugh. The fence extended out into the sea for several yards. Then it bent and ran along the seashore. Someone had faced this problem and solved it.

"It's not a metal I recognize, sir," said one man, examining the bars.

"Later." Zeras waved him away.

"It could be important," said the soldier, still examining the bars of the fence.

"We will explore later. We need to find those accursed people. And we must stay alive."

The path they trod had been treacherous. The land was crumbly and one had to take three steps to get one step farther. They had had to climb the steep range, which separated them from the inland areas. Now tired and footsore, they rested for an hour in a cave on the far side of the mountain.

"Something's happening," cried out a man, running into the cave. "Back!" he shouted.

The Autharians shrank back into the darkness while The Searing took place. Sometime later they looked out again and saw that all had returned to normal. Several miles away lay habitation.

Zeras held out his arm to stop his second from saying

anything further. He overheard voices. The men fell silent.

They watched as men, or anyway people resembling men, rolled by in chariots.

They paused and each took a sip of water. They looked out over the plain. "Remind me never to go hunting with you again," groused one man.

"It's not my fault I'm the best shot."

"You could miss occasionally to make us feel better," complained the other.

"When I am Emperor, I will pair you with someone as bad as yourself."

"Wonderful," crabbed the older man.

"Where do you go now?"

"Where else? To the Palace. There is not a minute to lose!"

When the chariots had rolled out of sight, Zeras and his man came out. "I think we've caught a break," observed Zeras thoughtfully.

"I wish you'd tell me how."

"All in good time, my dear Loogan," said he. And the Topsiders made their way down into the valley themselves.

The Gygax

The combat arena of Western Orcus was part of a larger entertainment complex a short distance from the Imperial Palace. In the morning, the humans had been provided with suitable clothing and taken to the armory. Here they were presented with an array of weapons.

Members of the Imperial Palace had accompanied the humans on this trip. It was considered part of the enjoyment to see which tools of war the combatants would select.

Mog walked beside the humans. Surrounding them was the Imperial Guard. Mog was larger than Otzi, broader, and yet just as dignified. Otzi found him sharp, intelligent, and not altogether friendly. The Emperor wore for the occasion a blue gown with epaulets and ceremonial armor. When they came to the armory, they greeted a squat, powerfully built figure who seemed ready to offer them advice about the weapons. Mog scrutinized the graceful lines of Artemis's physique and was affected. Such a human as this, he thought, would provide him with a long and attractive bloodline. Let them survive first, he thought, and then he'd consider it.

The racks presented an array of swords, shields, axes, and throwing knives. Lemnas confidently stepped up and took several knives. The guests in attendance admired the fearless youth.

Otzi surveyed the options. He had lost his sword in the battle with the finbacks. The metal with which these weapons were made did not look like bronze.

He lifted a sword. The weight also was different. It was a bit heavier but also felt more substantial. He swung it in the air. "What is this metal?"

The short man nodded. "You Topsiders do not have it. We call it 'steel.'"

"Impressive." Otzi nodded.

Ajax selected an axe and a short sword. He hoped that this would be enough.

"You have chosen well," said Zak to him.

The arena was filled with people. The Orcans did like their bloody battles to the death. This Gygax, the servant had explained to him, was the only one in captivity. They were difficult to ensnare—obviously—and this one was as strong as others. It had one distinguishing feature: it was narcoleptic.

"It falls asleep all of a sudden?" Otzi replied with astonishment, when the word had been explained to him.

"Not when fighting, unfortunately for you," assured him the servant. "Just when it's not worked up."

The arena was dug into a cliff face. It was an amphitheater facing a mountain. The designers had landscaped terrain to give the fighters some chance. In the middle of the space were several boulders behind which they could hide. There was a pillar for climbing. There was a pool of water and a bridge. They could perhaps take cover under the bridge for a moment.

The Thuringians entered by means of a heavy gate. The walls surrounding the arena were high and smooth. Neither the Gygax nor the humans would be climbing them or breaking down the gate.

A bank of musicians sat in their own section of the stands. They now played a flourish announcing the beginning of the event. Mog stood in the Imperial Box. He held up his hands. "Ladies and gentlemen," he cried out. "Orcans. Welcome!" The crowd shouted out its appreciation. "Today we have a rare treat. We have Topsiders! These gallant warriors have fought through many perils. I was moved by their tale of misfortune and laid aside the penalty of death reserved for humans entering our realm."

The people cheered at this show of clemency. Mog raised his hands again. "By the power vested in me, I am able to do this." He commenced to offer a legal justification for his actions. Otzi looked around. He saw, in the box next to Mog, Garo and Volney. They waved at him. Otzi nodded back and smiled.

It would be a pity, he thought, for the boy to see them die that day. He had no intention of letting that happen.

"Because of these factors, I have decided to act as I did," Mog concluded. "But enough of these long-winded explanations. You all have suffered enough!"

The audience laughed and clapped. Mog continued: "Let us see whether these Topsiders will live to fight another day. You all know that I could not make it easy for them. I present to you: The Gygax!"

There was a rumble of drums and another flourish of

trumpets. In the tunnel that led into the mountain, Ajax and Otzi could heard the lifting of a gate. They could hear the chain being pulled. The earth shook slightly. Then the Gygax stepped forward into the light.

Just as it came out, two of Artemis's arrows struck the creature in quick succession. One found its throat, while another impacted its chest. Whether because these were protected parts of its body, in contrast to that of a man, or because it was just that tough, the arrows hardly seemed to have an effect. The beast was fully eleven or twelve feet high, covered from head to foot in short, bluish-black fur. It resembled an ape—not that Otzi or the others had ever seen one. It was very powerfully built. Muscles rippled its chest, arms, and back. The arms were long and hung low to the ground, yet the creature walked upright on its hind legs. In its face the eyes were closely set, while its jaws could distend to reveal long, sharp incisor teeth. The beast glared about it fiercely.

Ajax had climbed atop one of the boulders. He challenged the creature, his weapons aloft. The Gygax was quick, quicker than Ajax expected. It rushed forward and swept its great arm at Ajax. Ajax leapt but still was caught with the blow. In falling he swung the axe and this slash caused the creature to draw back his hand. It had done the Gygax no damage, but had prevented it from grabbing Ajax's leg. The brawny mountaineer rolled back to his feet and ran to one side. Next the blue ape had to contend with some throwing knives. They seemed to vex him more than anything. He took two in the forearm and grunted. He pulled them out and, to everyone's surprise, threw them back at Lemnas. They were accurate too. They just missed, thudding into the wall of the arena. Artemis fired again to distract it. The Gygax was learning not to fear these arrows. It was assessing the enemy. It appeared to have decided to take them out one by one.

Otzi was the first target. The Gygax came rushing at him. Otzi tried slipping between the creature's legs. He had done this with the finback lizard but the ape was quicker. He halfway kicked Otzi, who grunted and was thrown aside. Just as he rose the Gygax was on him.

Otzi felt the unbelievable force of the creature's grip. It had him! What was he to do? Nothing. There was nothing to do. He looked up at the creature, who looked ferociously back. Its teeth were several inches long, and its breath was bad. He showed signs of intelligence but not of sympathy. His plan was to kill Otzi there and then.

The Thuringian leader felt one of his ribs snap. The pain was excruciating. There went another. The grip loosened. Ajax was on the thing's back. He had climbed up the pillar. This in itself was an amazing feat. Ajax had made use of several of Artemis's bowstrings. With this he had fashioned a simple lasso. When the crowd saw what he was planning, they cheered encouragingly. Garo cheered loudest of all.

Mog was impressed with these humans. They could almost account themselves warriors, he thought. Unfortunately for them it would all be over soon. The Gygax had the leader, Otzi. In Mog's experience, when the beast had its enemy in its powerful hug, it was all over. Without Otzi the group could no longer seriously hope to contend. The big man, Ajax, would run out of ideas and strength. The boy was quick but not going to do it. The old fellow was stashed under the bridge. *Was he their secret weapon?* he wondered with a sad flash of wit. Perhaps, if she survived to the last, Mog might be able to rescue Artemis. She would need time to get back her strength.

Her spirit would be affected by the defeat and also by the collapse of their plan. One never knew how people would respond. But in time, with encouragement and gifts, she might be brought back to a sociable state. If that were to happen, Mog would take her for his own.

Here, it was coming to it! He felt that thrill which accompanies the decisive moment in any contest. The audience also seemed to sense it. They grew still, their lips parted slightly in anticipation. The Emperor, Mog, leaned forward to get a better view.

Konno's Revolt

Konno and his allies had returned to their palaces in the wealthier districts of town. This was a moment for which they had long prepared. The appearance of these humans had been a stroke of good fortune for the Orcan Emperor, but it would not avail him in the long run.

Their forces were considerable. For generations they had ruled Orcus. This upstart had taken advantage of temporary conditions to assert control. Now was when the tables would be turned.

Konno was the most prominent member of this conspiracy. The leaders gathered in his garden. There they all were: powerful, large limbed and intelligent, a force of Neanderthals to be reckoned with. They went down into the cellar of the house. Konno brought them to a wall. He reached for a brick in the wall. It was loose. He pulled it slowly out and tossed it aside. He nodded to the soldiers, who began to pull out the other bricks. In a couple of minutes they had opened up a walkway. There was a tunnel behind it. This tunnel would bring them to the Imperial Palace.

Zeras had followed with interest the progress of the aristocratic Orcans. He took care to remain, with his troops, under the cover of foliage. They moved swiftly, for Zeras worked only with the best. They kept some distance from the city which Konno approached.

They did not want to be spotted. As the day faded, he told them to get ready. Zeras had no interest in Orcan politics. But if there was to be a period of civil strife, they might take advantage. Zeras could feel the end of this chase approaching.

Otzi's vision began to grow dim. The Gygax was holding him in a crushing embrace. He looked upward and saw a shadow. Ajax had used the lasso of bowstrings to clamber up the pillar in the middle of the arena. From here he launched himself down onto the back of the Gygax.

The Gygax roared and spun around, still holding Otzi. With one hand Ajax swung the axe. This time there was blood, and quite a lot of it. But the slash did not seem to inflict a fatal wound upon the creature. It let go of Otzi and reached up to grab Ajax. This time it managed to grab the man's leg. Otzi stumbled out of range and looked for his weapon. Powerful as ever; the Gygax swung Ajax fully against the boulder. Ajax felt the wind knocked out of him. He was not sure if there was anything else wrong. He felt numb on one side, which was never good. Otzi stabbed the creature in the stomach. The beast seemed to feel this as a mere irritation. Next it was Lemnas's turn. He leapt from the rock onto the creature's back. He slashed it with the knife but without much damage. He somersaulted off again.

The great ape was not yet seriously hurt. It was, however, seriously annoyed. The crowd cheered throughout. Ajax had stumbled to his feet. Still holding his side, he got behind a rock. The Gygax tried another strategy. It lurched out into the open. It felt that it had a good chance if the little men were on the floor. Don't let them leap down from boulders and pillars!

The audience that rooted for the monster tried to warn it of the humans' plan. They shouted, they pointed. The Gygax became aware of these shouts. It did not see quite what the crowd was referring to. Suddenly it felt an immense bang on its head and the world fell dark.

Otzi, peerless strategist from the lofty Alps Mountains on the Topside, had thought long and hard about how to defeat the creature. They had asked for information about the arena. It came to the Thuringians with only a couple of hours to go. They would deploy Nestor! The old man would hide under the bridge until the fight was well under way. With the creature distracted, he would steal out and initiate the plan. Nestor was past his prime as a fighting man. Nevertheless, after years of scrapping, he still retained his strength. Nestor crouched down. They were next to the entrance to the tunnel from which the beast had emerged. Artemis, leaning one hand against the cliff face, stepped onto Nestor's shoulders. With a groan

Nestor rose from the squatting position. Artemis was now just about high enough. She leapt up and grabbed with one hand the lintel of the entranceway. With agonizing effort she pulled herself up. There was a narrow protrusion of hewn stones up there. She commenced to loosen one of the large stones, which rested above the lintel.

The trick now was to maneuver the Gygax within range. Nestor meanwhile had hidden himself away again. The Gygax had come to hate the boulders. He would hate the tunnel entrance even more. As he stepped back for unobstructed space, the young warrior girl, Artemis, rolled the stone over.

The Gygax would have a terrible headache when it awoke.

The humans, still battered and sore, appeared before Mog in the Hall of Festivities. They stood, weapons in hand, facing the Emperor of Western Orcus. The event had had the quality of a popular festival. In front the Emperor had walked with various palace dignitaries. Behind them, still flanked by the Palace Guard, were these victorious warriors. In the next row walked their advocates, Garo and his guardian. For the occasion they had provided a wheelchair for his Volney. One of the Guards wheeled the old man along.

They entered the Hall of Festivities. The audience had gathered as well. The Emperor raised his hand again and all fell silent. "Congratulations, Topsiders. Artemis, Otzi, Nestor, Ajax, and Lemnas. You have exceeded even my lofty expectations."

"Our thanks to you, Sire," replied Otzi with a gracious

smile. "Had you not made the decision to grant us clemency, we would not be at this stage."

"Bring forth the laurels of victory!" commanded Mog.

Just as this was about to take place, a throng of newcomers stepped forward from the side. "Not so fast!" said they.

Mog was taken aback. "Konno!" he cried.

"Yes, it is I, Konno. How clever of you to order this proceeding while the rest of us were out of the capital."

"It's not my responsibility," shrugged Mog, with a glint of triumph in his eye. "And anyway, don't you know when you're not wanted?"

The crowd, fresh from the spectacle of this great contest, shouted in irritation. They had not failed to notice, however, that the men who now stood up front were armed.

"We do not allow this ceremony to take place. Topsiders, when they enter Orcus, die. It's just that simple."

"Not in this case," replied Mog tersely.

"In every case," countered Konno.

"It seems to me, Konno, that you are getting a little big for your britches."

"Emperor Mog, you have behaved in ways contrary to the best interests of Western Orcus. We can no longer allow you to remain in power."

"We will see about that," replied Mog haughtily, and drew his sword.

Otzi and his friends watched with disbelief as this scene was unfolding. Mayhem was about to ensue. The crowd was becoming panicked and sought to exit. The Palace Guards stepped out of the way to avoid being trampled.

"This way! I know the way!" It was Garo. Mog turned to them. "Yes, you! Boy." "Garo," corrected the boy with composure and dignity.

"Garo, yes," Mog corrected himself. "Show them the way. Otzi, my friends, you see how it is."

"We do, Mog, and thanks."

"Go now! Say hello to the Topside for me." Mog offered them a rueful smile. He turned to the fight at hand.

Fight at the Geyser

Garo did not know the Palace well, but he knew the mountain behind it. They crossed a walkway and garden. Neanderthals were running back and forth in panic. The path led into the mountain. No one was watching it. Garo and his Topside friends rushed into the dark, cavernous complex.

Magnificently carved tunnels branched off in all directions. Stairs carved in rock led upward, they led downward. The little Neanderthal boy knew the way. After about a mile the tunnels became less polished. They entered through a heavy wooden door. They went down some stairs.

Then they opened another door. They heard rushing water. At the end of this tunnel was Zeras. They walked forward to where the Autharian stood.

"You imagined you were going to escape, did you?" he asked with a triumphant smirk.

"I may have," replied Otzi, shaking his head. He paused. "I have to give you credit."

"Thanks just the same. Well, look, we could engage in a lot of charming banter but I'd rather just fight. I have some guys. You have some guys. Put that to one side."

"I just fought a twelve-foot furry beast."

"Not my problem." Zeras shrugged and unsheathed his sword. To one side stood Zeras's men. Their weapons were drawn, to the other the Thuringians and Garo. In the middle was a pond with some curious-looking plants. They resembled lilies.

Otzi removed his sword too. He felt, as he did so, the rasp of his broken ribs. He wasn't sure about this one.

"Broken ribs," Zeras nodded. "I can tell."

"I won't make it easy for you," Otzi assured him. The two warriors clashed back and forth. Zeras was a very accomplished warrior. On the other hand, Otzi had had a lot of practice of late. Zeras slashed Otzi on the arm, but as they passed, Otzi clocked him with his forearm. They switched places and faced each other again.

Ajax was relatively sure he could take three or four of these soldiers. Artemis could account for two more. Lemnas could take one and maybe Nestor also at a stretch. The problem was the ten remaining. The fight continued down the hallway. The attention of the men was drawn to the fight. The combatants were exerting themselves to the fullest.

Ajax, in the corner of his eye, noticed that Garo was doing something curious. He was raking the circular pool for lilies. Why was he doing that?

Otzi was getting the worst of these exchanges. He hated to admit it, but this Zeras was an expert fighter. However, Otzi had an idea. It was such a good idea that he had to force himself not to smile.

"I can't even see why you still try," taunted Zeras. "We have gotten past the point where you could win."

"Hmm. It's in my nature," blustered Otzi.

"You're a stubborn buzzard, I'll give you that."

"Mountain tough," rejoined Otzi with a flash of a grin.

"I'll be wrapping quickly now, I think." Zeras redoubled his attack. He was well rested. He was accomplished. He had much experience.

It was his weapon that was the problem. Otzi remembered, in the middle of the fight, that his sword was a little different from the Autharian's. It was an Orcan sword. The metal was stronger. The armorer, Zak, had called it "steel." Zeras slashed at Otzi, narrowly missing his stomach. It was here that Otzi launched his final, desperate attack. Though it caused him much pain to his ribs, Otzi slashed with all his might. Zeras blocked the blow. The Autharian's sword chipped out. Before he could change positions Otzi slashed again and again. Zeras's sword was made of bronze. It could not resist the other. His sword snapped in half and Otzi cut him across the chest. Zeras's men stepped forward in alarm.

"That's Orcan steel for you," declared Otzi. Zeras looked at his broken sword with disbelief. For the first time in years something like apprehension came into his face. Otzi took several steps and launched into a flying leap. He kicked the Autharian captain back into the geyser. The man was swept away in a second. He was out of sight. He was gone.

Ajax saw what Otzi had done. Unsheathing his sword, he swept into Zeras's men. Rattled by the loss of their leader, the soldiers were slow to respond. They could not meet the flashing fury of Ajax's steel axe blade. Several fell. Two more were pierced with arrows and lay there, heaving. The rest were overcome by the absence of any prospect of escape. For even if they got away from these mountain terrors, what then? They were in the realm of Orcus.

At sword point Otzi led the captives into a side chamber. Garo assured them that they would be going nowhere. Ajax jammed the broken stub of Zeras's sword between the door handles. They were locked in.

Topside Once More

"Garo, which way out of here?" Otzi asked their young friend smilingly.

"The geyser," Garo pointed at the vertical stream of water.

"How does that work exactly?"

"This will take you Topside. This will take you close to your home."

"Just like that?" They grinned.

"Not exactly," replied Garo. He reached for a rake. Slowly, carefully, he pulled the lilies in the pond closer to them. As with many things in Orcus, these lilies had no exact match in the world above. Garo carefully lifted the flower up. Under it was what looked like a seedpod. Delicately he pulled it off its stem. He wanted to avoid tearing it. Next, he found the seam of the pod and opened it. Inside were perhaps a dozen large green seeds.

"Delicious," joked Nestor.

Garo held up the pod. "This pod does not grow in the Topside. It only grows down here. It is very useful because it helps you breathe. The journey to the Topside takes longer than you have breath. Here, I will show you."

Garo held the open pod up to his face. He smoothed the seam of it above his nose and below his mouth. The edges of the pod had some kind of sticky or catchy surface. When Garo pressed them together, they stayed pressed. They watched as he breathed in and out. They nodded and murmured their approval.

"This pod will hold thirty breaths. You will need almost all of them."

"Garo, our great thanks," said Otzi simply. He shook the boy's hand. They all did in turn.

"You go now," he said, gesturing at the geyser. "Hold your head down so that the pod does not come off."

"Right," said Ajax. "Me first."

"You will be all right?" Otzi asked. He did not want to leave the boy to get into trouble.

"Yes, it is fine," said the boy.

"Here I go!" Ajax had put the pod over his face. He plunged into the geyser. In a second he was gone.

"I'm next!" declared Lemnas. He followed.

"No, it's me!" insisted Nestor pettishly when Artemis was reaching for a pod.

"Well, all right then," retorted Artemis in irritation. After Nestor she went up. Next Otzi, with one final nod, jumped into the surging water.

The water bubbled and rushed about him. Otzi continued to look down. His breath came fast and short. He was afraid of what might happen. The water began to have a soothing effect. The seed pod worked perfectly. Water did not even leak through to his mouth. His breathing steadied and he opened his eyes. The water around him was dark. He enjoyed the surge of its resistless power. He began to notice some glimmer of gray around him. Still it was dim, yet gradually it grew brighter. Suddenly it became much brighter. He risked looking up. He could see a pool of light far above. He was close now. He was— through!

The bright blue sky of the Topside shone all around him. He was blinded for a moment by the whiteness of the clouds. He was in a lake he knew well. He had been here a hundred times in his life—no, more. He laughed and coughed and looked about him. His friends had waded to shore and were lying on the beach. About them were the mountains of his home country. They were not far. The snowbound peaks shone distantly down upon him. Otzi paddled to dry land.

The others said nothing. They lay there, panting and trying to gather themselves. The sun was warm but they knew they could not rest. None of this would have meant anything if the traveling party returned too late. After a minute, they nodded at each other. Without a word they climbed to their feet and jogged down the walking path.

The path led down a steep hillside and across the shoulder of a hill. They came to a rocky outcrop overlooking the Thurin valley. One glance was sufficient to tell them all. They were not too late, and neither were they too early. They were just in time. They pulled back from the edge. They must not reveal themselves yet.

The five friends scuttered swiftly across the top of the ridge. Otzi had a plan in mind, and the others instinctively understood it. Once they had reached the spot, they looked carefully over. Down below they saw the strong contingent of Trilock's men. These men numbered fully seventy or eighty. They looked to be accomplished warriors. They marched upon the entrance to the town. The redoubtable Thuringian villagers opposed them. The scouts at least had given Otzi's countrymen some warning. Even so, as the matter stood, the villagers were up against it.

The villagers fired a volley of arrows. The Autharian henchmen were ready for it. No more than two of these men fell. The villagers launched another volley. This time one man fell. The henchmen walked patiently forward.

Otzi stepped back from the edge. He considered what they had to work with. "There," he said, pointing to an enormous boulder, which stood, poised precariously, near the edge of the cliff.

"Be like crushing Gygaxes," commented Artemis humorously.

"Do it in one's sleep," seconded Ajax with a grin.

They loosened the stone in front. "Not yet," warned Nestor, who was watching the men below. "All right... now." They pushed.

⚔

The leader of the Autharians walked determinedly forward. Now they almost had done it. The journey up to these heights had been long. Each man was a tried warrior and there were few complaints. These men, the leader knew, were troubled more by their memories than by the task ahead. In past times, such men as these had fought for beliefs, in devotion to their tribal lord. They had even fought for love. Now they all were beyond that. They fought now because they were good at it, and because it meant a substantial payday. Their task was to roust out these simple villagers. When he thought of these people, the leader felt a surge of impatience. They should have known better than to resist. The force Trilock had assembled was several times the strength and size of these uplanders. When people insisted on taking foolish positions, misfortune tended to befall them. The time of the Thuringians was at an end.

He felt the change before it occurred. He felt against his weathered cheek some brief mouth of wind. The mountain, the boulder. The stentorian rumble of that piece of earth could be felt for miles around. Its speed was too quick for thought. *I am dead,* thought the leader, as the crushing tons of weight broke his body. *Well done.*

Homecoming

Otzi surveyed the crushed trees, the pulverized branches, the prone, trembling bodies below. Still he was not satisfied. He urged the others to push over more, and they did. These two found their mark. Now the villagers mounted an attack. Trilock's men were forced to retreat. The dead they left where they lay. Ajax led the way down the path along the cliff. It was fully half an hour before they came to the valley floor.

The villagers grinned at them victoriously and nodded. They embraced and cheered. They looked inquiringly at the travelers, certain that their journey had yielded a couple of tales.

Lemnas was embraced by his family and Ajax by his friends. Nestor clapped his nephews and daughter in his arms. Artemis walked the hills in quiet communion with her friends. The mountains were still there, and Thurin Village was still intact.

Otzi settled into the heavy leather chair of his living room. The main room was warm from the fire. He sat with a cup of warm tea and contemplated his many bruises and aches. He could feel his ribs, and his face still smarted from many blows. He smiled at his wife and child.

His boy looked up at him eagerly. "What happened, Daddy?' he asked. "Did you fall down?"

"Nope," replied Otzi. "Never yet."

His wife, Ana, was warming up a cauldron of stew. "All right," she said sternly. "No more adventures for a while."

"Not a problem. Yes," said Otzi with an easy grin.

Ana looked at him more sternly still. "I'm serious. That's it."

"Agreed," replied Otzi with a grateful smile. "I'm going to take a load off," said he.

Above the clustered huts of the Thurin Village, the evening was darkening into night. The residents were finishing their meals, but soon they might decide to go for a walk. The jagged outline of Mount Aalok rose above the valley. It was a dark outline against the sky. Soon, however, the moon would be rising and bathing the valley in her silvery light. The glittering beams would shine coldly upon the mountain peaks, while in the valley residents might walk almost as if it were day. The Thuringian relaxed in their homes. They had fulfilled their sacred obligations. They had attended the Ceremonial Kula, and they had given their sacred gift. The Goddess Perchta mounted aloft in her mighty chariot. The mountain people might feel at ease for another year at least.

About the Author

 **BUD SELIGSON** is the product of Chicago, Illinois. He received his bachelor's degree at the University of Illinois–Navy Pier Branch. His love of history, both ancient and modern, led him to Northwestern University's Special Historical Studies. The terrible Chicago winters found him quickly heading to the warmer climate offered by Southern California, where along with his wife and often co-author, Diane, they moved into a most interesting line of work in and out of several movie studios. For many years, Bud worked as a ghostwriter and story doctor to several famous authors whose names are extremely well known! Bud has teamed up within the last year with the famous second writer for *Gilligan's Island, Scooby Doo, Laverne and Shirley*, etc., etc. His partner's well-known name in the industry is Ron Sellz, and together they have just completed nine new novels that should be in print for early 2017. Bud is the father of two and grandfather of seven. Thank you for the read.

www.ingramcontent.com/pod-product-compliance
Lightning Source LLC
Chambersburg PA
CBHW020120180626
46812CB00006B/2678